J. Auchinleck.

2 Castle Street

CRAIL.

Stewart Auchinleck

THE
GLOBE
RESTORED

THE
GLOBE RESTORED

A STUDY OF THE
ELIZABETHAN THEATRE
BY C. WALTER HODGES

ERNEST BENN LIMITED ❖ LONDON

First published 1953

PUBLISHED BY ERNEST BENN LIMITED
BOUVERIE HOUSE · FLEET STREET · LONDON · EC4
PRINTED IN GREAT BRITAIN

TO

RICHARD SOUTHERN

Preface

THE GLOBE Theatre, which was once a commonplace of the London riverside, and stood in ordinary sun and rain, and grew shabby and had new coats of paint from time to time, and was visited by thousands of people as people nowadays visit the greyhound track or the cinema, has gone forever. Some of its timbers were doubtless sawn up for firewood, some used in the building of other houses, and some two or three, removed again, remain perhaps even to this day built into the wall of a gentleman's week-end cottage in Surrey. But now that the old theatre has been so long demolished, it turns out that there are very few historical buildings of which we would so much wish to have had a reliable record. The problem of reconstructing it has become a fascinating exercise in the field of literary conjecture, the more especially since it is probable that the exact truth about it can never now be known, and that beyond the point where evidence leaves off there is some need, and considerable stimulus, for the imagination. In this book I have tried to strike a proper and declared balance between the facts and my own interpretation of them. No one, I think, is justified in offering a reconstruction of an Elizabethan theatre without insisting upon the necessarily conjectural nature of much of it, in view of the limited evidence now available; but if with this caution in mind the reader chooses to accept my findings here, I believe he will find himself somewhere not far from the truth.

I am indebted to many helpers, most particularly to my friend Richard Southern who has allowed me the use not only of his collection of books and pictures but of his researches also, which is generosity indeed. I would like also to acknowledge my thanks to Mr. Walter H. Godfrey, a pioneer in the reconstruction of Elizabethan theatres, who has given me valuable help and advice on many occasions; to Mr. James Laver who has helped me greatly at the Victoria and Albert Museum; to Professor Allardyce Nicoll who as editor of *Shakespeare Survey* first published the article which now appears, with modification, as Chapter 3; and to Bernard and Josephine Miles, in whose garden-house in St. John's Wood many of the pictures in this book were first shown as an exhibition which they helped me to arrange in connexion with the first season of their Mermaid Theatre. I also wish to express thanks to my wife, who has fed, housed and endured this hobby-horse of mine for some years, and has at last groomed it, typed it, and helped me to send it out into the world.

Among the many books I have consulted, I wish to acknowledge my particular debt to the writings of W. J. Lawrence (*The Physical Features of the Elizabethan Playhouse*, and *Pre-Restoration Stage Studies*); to G. R. Reynolds' *Staging of Elizabethan Plays at the Red Bull Theatre*, which in my view has not yet been equalled as a work of close interpretative analysis on the subject; to John Cranford Adams' *The Globe Theatre, its Design and Equipment*; to George R. Kernodle's *From Art to Theatre*; and of course to the four invaluable volumes of Sir E. K. Chambers' *The Elizabethan Stage*. And being conscious of all the earlier work by other men, I can only offer as my excuse for coming in at this point the following, from John Speed's Preface to his *Theatre of the Empire of Great Britain*:—

> *I stand in suspense, so many maister-builders having in this subject gone before me, and I the least, not worthy to hew (much less to lay) the least stone in so beautiful a Building; neither can I for my heedless presumption alledge any excuse, unless it be this, that . . . I knew not what I undertook until I saw the charges thereof by others bestowed to amount so high as I held it a conscience to frustrate their designments; wherein albeit it may be objected I have put my sickle into other men's corn and have laid my building upon other men's foundations . . . yet this in part sufficeth for my defence, that in the work of the Tabernacle there was more mettals used than orient gold, and more workmen employed than Aholiab and Bezaleel.*

Bishopstone, 1953   C. W. H.

Contents

List of Illustrations

The Plates inserted as pages 121–168

xi

Line Drawings in the Text

Drawings by the Author

1. The Ruins of Palmyra

FOR the space of a generation, from the latter half of the reign of Elizabeth the First until the time of the Civil War, there flourished in London no less than fourteen theatres. Some of these, calling themselves private theatres, were built indoors for the comfortable entertainment of fairly small but select audiences; but the rest, nine altogether, were public places built rather like small Roman amphitheatres, open to the sky, and each capable of holding about two thousand spectators. Nothing quite like them had been known in Europe since the days of the Roman Empire, and not for more than another two hundred years was there any other city which could show so many permanent theatres at one time. The name of one of these will remain illustrious so long as there is any history of theatres at all. It is that of Shakespeare's theatre, the Globe.

We have details of more than twenty actors' companies who worked in the theatres of Elizabethan and Jacobean London, and of these nearly five hundred

15

individual actors are known to us by name—some, like Alleyn, Burbage, Field, Armin, Kempe and Tarlton, by much more than name. We know, from the documents that have come down to us, much detail of their management and organisation, of their legal and business affairs, and especially of their plays. Wide and crowded shelves make up the library of surviving Elizabethan plays, good, bad and brilliant, from the pens of more than a dozen famous dramatists, without counting Marlowe, Jonson or Shakespeare. If the theatres were the first of their kind since Roman times, there had been nothing to compare with this fountain of playwriting since the days of Periclean Athens. It is therefore the more remarkable that with all this residue of fame and knowledge to guide us, we are to-day more uncertain about the actual stagecraft employed in the original production of one of Shakespeare's plays at the Globe than we are of any other event of comparable importance in the whole history of the theatre.

This is not to say that we know nothing: we know much about it—but it is widely believed that we know much more than we do; for where knowledge ends conjecture has been accepted to fill the unacceptable gap.

Knowledge on the subject is most extensive over its peripheral areas. For example, we are pretty well informed about audiences at the Globe and how they behaved there, or about the cost of an actor's wardrobe, or of getting a poet released from prison, and so on. It is when we seek for reliable information about the centre of all this, the stage itself and how it was used, that the evidence suddenly becomes obscure on many points, and on others is altogether lacking. For example, there are in existence authentic contracts which give what at first appear to be full details for the building of two of the theatres, the Fortune and the Hope; but the Hope contract, when it comes to the point where it should describe the stage, which is the thing above all which we wish to have described, tells us nothing except that it was built on trestles so that it could easily be taken down; and the Fortune contract, having stated that the details of its stage are to be copied from the Globe, at that point purports to append a diagram of it, to make all clear. That diagram, alas, has not survived. Had it done so, it might have saved a whole world of ink and paper which has since tried to reconstruct it.

It is my purpose in this book to bring together a collection of evidence, and especially of pictures related to the subject, which, together with some personal opinions and reconstructions of my own, will create a visual impression of the style and manner of the London theatre in the time of Shakespeare. And since for most people to-day this means the Globe, we shall do well to take the Globe for the centre and model of our subject.

There were two versions of the Globe. The first was built on Bankside in Southwark in 1599, and enjoyed a successful career until 1613, when it was accidentally burned down during a play which, from its description, we take to be Shakespeare's *Henry VIII*. The second was built to replace it on the same site, and was opened the following year. The management took the occasion to improve on their former building, and a certain John Chamberlain wrote in a letter to a friend that he heard 'much speech of this new playhouse, which is said to be the fairest that ever was in England'. This second building continued on Bankside until 1644, when, what with the ground-lease falling in, the Civil War in progress, the Puritans in the ascendant and the old theatres out of fashion anyway, it was finally pulled down. Its near neighbour, which had once been the Hope theatre, but which had long since reverted to an older calling as a bear-baiting arena, survived it for a few more years, the last of the old colony of amphitheatres on Bankside. It was demolished in 1656. Its site is still marked by an alley called Bear Gardens; and next door to it is another, Rose Alley, which marks the site of a yet older theatre, the Rose. The Globe stood a short way to the east and south of this, and the whole group, as it existed in 1600, can be seen in a newly discovered revised version of Norden's map of London, the Bankside portion of which is shown in Plate 2. This is now considered to be the most reliable of all the old maps of Bankside, but even so the Rose is wrongly named in it, being here called the Star. The mistake may have arisen because a heraldic rose, if seen indistinctly, could easily be confused with a heraldic star. The mistake is in any case typical of many which have confused research on the siting of these theatres. There is no room here to describe the difficulties which for a long time obstructed the search for the lost site of the Globe itself, but it is relevant to note that in the course of it it was necessary to establish, firstly, that an old map, vital to the evidence, had actually been drawn upside down, and secondly, that in a famous engraving, Hollar's *Long View of London*, which shows the Globe and the Bear-garden as they were shortly before the Civil War (Plate 4), the titles of these two theatres had accidentally been interchanged, the Globe being named 'Beere bayting' and vice versa. The site of the Globe has now been established beyond reasonable doubt, and those two unlikely-seeming propositions have been proved to be correct; but it can well be imagined that many experts found them difficult to accept, and that research was confused as a consequence.

A similar confusion and controversy still exists as to the actual shape of the Globe. Shakespeare called it a 'wooden O', but it is contended that if it

B

had been a fully rounded O it was not likely, for structural reasons, to have been made all of wood. It is possible that the outer wall was circular, composed of some sort of flint and mortar concrete, and that it contained an inner polygonal structure of timber galleries. Hollar's engraving certainly shows a smooth round exterior, though other engravings show it externally as a polygon (cf. Visscher's engraving, Plate 1). It seems probable to me that it was a wooden polygon of so many sides, sixteen for example, that from any distance it would have appeared as a full round, and that Hollar, making the original sketch for his engraving from the tower of what is now Southwark Cathedral, would have found it most convenient to draw it so (Plate 5). But whatever doubts there may be about this detail, there ought to be none about the quality of Hollar's picture as a whole. It is the only single picture of the Bankside playhouses which we can confidently accept as a good and reliable representation. The only question is whether there had been any substantial alterations made between Shakespeare's time and the time when Hollar made his drawing. There is no real reason to suppose there had been.

As soon as regular playgoing was resumed in London at the Restoration, the old-time theatres were remembered with some contempt. 'Now for the difference between our Theatres and those of former times', wrote one Restoration commentator,[1] 'they were but plain and simple, with no Scenes, nor Decorations of the Stage, but onely old Tapestry, and the Stage strewed with rushes, (with their Habits accordingly)'. This was the view of the Elizabethan theatre which was to prevail for more than two hundred years thereafter, that it was a poor barnyard affair, picturesque but crude. The rush-strewn stage and the lack of movable picture-scenery could not help but seem a great drawback to the new generation of playgoers for whom the splendid scenic inventions which had been introduced into this country by Inigo Jones a generation before, at the court of James I, were now being shown regularly on the public stage. 'Scenes' were the rage, and such of the Elizabethan plays as were thought suitable for revival were now altered to suit the scenic style. Shakespeare's were among the first to be adapted. Pepys wrote in his diary that he had been to see 'Hamlet done with scenes very well'. So the old theatres had gone, not only unregretted but unremembered. Moreover, they had suffered the fate of so many commonplace and popular institutions, that everybody had taken them for granted and nobody had put them on record. Such inadequate records as we have date from their early days, when

---

[1] Richard Flecknoe, *Discourse of the English Stage*, 1664.

they were novelties; but of their later professional and routine years we have not much record at all.

There remained, however, the printed plays, especially the plays of Shakespeare, and as time went on it began to be necessary for editors to explain those technical peculiarities which, under the now well-settled system of the scenic theatre, seemed increasingly ill suited to what had become the normal stage requirements. For example, how had Shakespeare intended the rapid succession of short scenes in Act IV of *Antony and Cleopatra* to be presented? Or what does Cassius mean in Act V of *Julius Caesar* when he instructs Pindarus to 'get higher on that hill'? And when *Pindarus goes up*, up on what in fact does he go? Then in *Henry VIII*, II, ii, after a scene between the Lord Chamberlain and the Dukes of Norfolk and Suffolk, a stage direction says *Exit Lord Chamberlain; and the King draws the curtain and sits reading pensively;* but what curtain is referred to here? The 'doors' which are often alluded to, as in *Cymbeline*, VII, where *Enter . . . the Roman Army at one door and the Briton Army at another* might perhaps make sense to an eighteenth-century reader whose stage still contained, by tradition, two fixed doors in the proscenium; but none the less he would have thought it a curious use of such doors. But then turning from Shakespeare to Field's *A Woman's a Weathercock*, the eighteenth-century reader might be even more hard put to it to make sense out of the stage direction *Scudmore passeth one door and entereth the other, where Bellafront sits in a Chair, under a Taffeta Canopy.* Such references to contemporary stage conditions could perhaps be explained away as the quaint makeshifts of a bygone age, but even so it was not altogether clear what they were making shift to do.

Meanwhile certain old engravings of Bankside had been copied and copied again, one from another, and the strange tub-shaped buildings which were to be seen in the foregrounds of most of them became stranger and stranger as the debasement of copies went on (cf. Plates 8 and 9). Antiquarians and literary people in the eighteenth century puzzled over them; but if ever they went over to Bankside in search of grounds more relevant than this, they must have been disappointed; though Mrs. Thrale indeed believed that she had seen the actual remains of the Globe itself. Her husband, Henry Thrale, had established his brewery on Bankside upon a site which is still occupied by a famous brewery to-day, and which, according to local tradition at that time, included the site of the Globe. Mrs. Thrale wrote of it afterwards, in her memoirs:

'For a long time, then—or I thought it such—my fate was bound up with the old Globe Theatre, upon the Bankside, Southwark; the alley it had occupied having been purchased and thrown down by Mr Thrale to make an opening before the windows of our dwelling-house. When it lay desolate in a black heap of rubbish, my Mother, one day, in a joke, called it the Ruins of Palmyra; and after that they laid it down in a grass-plot. Palmyra was the name it went by, I suppose, among the clerks and servants of the brewhouse. . . . But there were really curious remains of the old Globe Playhouse, which though hexagonal in form without, was round within.'

Yet she was wrong, after all. Her Palmyra was not the ruin of the Globe, but of some old tenements a little way off to the south of it, which were demolished in 1767, just about the time she went to live in Southwark. As for the true site, she and her husband must have walked over it in the brewery many times. Her observations about the shape of the Globe, hexagonal without and round within, are open to doubt on many grounds, and one must suppose she was quoting from a studious mixture of Shakespeare's 'wooden O' speech and the Visscher engraving.

But though the Globe was lost there were certain critics in the latter part of the eighteenth century who, in spite of the well-developed amenities of the theatres of their own time, were prepared to believe that the stagecraft of Shakespeare's day deserved investigation. In the Introduction to his 1768 edition of Shakespeare, Edward Capell wrote: 'Even the stage he [Shakespeare] appeared upon, its form, dressings, actors should be enquired into, as every one of those circumstances had some considerable effect upon what he composed for it.' This suggestion was taken up by Edmund Malone a few years later, and it was he whose researches into the Henslowe documents, the Revels accounts and other contemporary records, laid the foundations upon which all the subsequent work of reconstruction was based.

Throughout the nineteenth century the features of the lost Globe were diligently hunted in texts and documents, and, where these failed, in the light of conjectural inspiration. The study of it, so rich in colour and so fruitful of interesting detail, proved to be as baffling as it was attractive. However, an answer was provided bit by bit, and if we now think that it erred too far upon the side of the primitive, this was only in keeping with the then prevailing belief in the general progress of cultured man out of medieval backwardness towards Victorian enlightenment. Besides, the evidence of the condition of the Elizabethan theatre did much to confirm this view. What else could one think of a theatre where the roof was of thatch, and where, while a part of the audience was expected to stand on a winter's afternoon under an open sky, another part was allowed to sit smoking and playing cards upon the stage, interrupting the play at will? And had not Shakespeare himself described his theatre as 'a cockpit', a 'wooden O' and an 'unworthy scaffold', lamenting the conditions which were to reduce his Agincourt to the scale of 'four or five most vile and ragged foils right ill-disposed in brawl ridiculous'? If such, then, were really the customs of the Elizabethan playhouse (and no one suggests that they were not, though we may wonder to what degree they applied) it is fair to ask whether it has been worth while to take so much trouble to reconstruct so simple a thing. But the point is that it has always been suspected, and for good reasons, that the evidence that has survived, unassailable though it is as to detail within the subject, is in fact not typical of the character of the subject as a whole: it is very much concerned with picturesque oddities which were noted at the time simply because they were odd and picturesque. The work of research has been to find the truth which lay behind them.

The desire to collect and restore the relics of past time, to re-create the features of history, to establish and guard them in the air-conditioned permanence of libraries, museums and art galleries, is one of the characteristic impulses of our age. It is, I suppose, a form of ancestor-worship. It seems to promise us the security of our own memorials in the future, since the tribute which we thus pay to our forefathers we may expect to be repaid to ourselves, when our time comes to be forefathers. The piecing-together of the Globe is only a part of the general piecing-together which, from the days of the eighteenth-century antiquarians until now, has thoroughly restored to us a whole world of reference of our past. It has been found all the more exasperating, therefore, that considering the veneration given to Shakespeare, it has been so difficult to collect the working details of his stage—or, for that matter, of his own life. This has not only been a goad to research, but provides, moreover, its own pleasures in the game of conjectural detection. But there is more to it than this. The relics and curiosities which former antiquaries collected, are now seen for what they are: not, that is, as 'curiosities' at all, but as mature examples of artistic styles which, although they may be unlike our own, are usually every inch as good, and sometimes better. So it is with the Elizabethan theatre. I do not think it can be claimed that as a theatre it was any better than our own, though in most respects it was as good. The question of comparative quality is not the point, however. The point is that the presentations of the Elizabethan theatre were expressed in an artistic style which was different from ours, and was largely abandoned in favour of the scenery theatre, not because it was essentially inferior to it, but because the scenery theatre had all the glamour of aristocratic taste and of magic novelty to back it up. This has now been developed to the point where further progress is hardly to be imagined. The Elizabethan style, however, still remains to be explored and developed from where it left off, and contains, fully ripened and ready for planting, the seeds of a different kind of theatrical experience from the one we are accustomed to. It is because of its abiding artistic potency that people in the theatre, ever since Benjamin Webster's attempt in 1844 to reconstruct the original staging of *The Taming of the Shrew*, and especially since the famous experiments of William Poel and his company at the St. George's Hall in 1881 and with the Elizabethan Stage Society thereafter, have so often been ready to try putting the Elizabethan method into practice; and it has been for this reason rather more than for the picturesque braggadocio of its historical colour that the restoration of the Globe has been so much advocated. But what has still to be decided is the character which such a restoration ought to have.

TIR ING HOUSE
Details not
known

Entry
?

Entry
?

2. Some Problems of Reconstruction

I HAVE suggested already that the Victorian belief in straight-line progress from the Middle Ages onwards had led to over-simplification in the problem of the Globe. It has led, among other things, to the assumption that our modern kind of theatre originated in the Elizabethan one; and this being so, it was supposed that by tracing backwards from eighteenth-century and Restoration theatres one would find their embryonic form at the Globe. This in its turn has led to a belief, which is to be discussed in the next chapter, that the modern proscenium arch developed out of the Elizabethan 'inner stage'. But even that 'inner stage' itself is more of a nineteenth-century supposition than an Elizabethan fact. According to W. J. Lawrence, it was first suggested by Ludwig Tieck, the great German editor and translator of Shakespeare, in the course of a historical novel. The trouble about the straight-line-progress idea was that it did not take into account the possibility that the Restoration stage was arrived at more by deliberate invention than by historical development, and that the Elizabethan public theatre was principally the repository of a great medieval tradition of stagecraft which was not handed on, but fizzled out on Bankside in the years after Shakespeare's death, while the new stagecraft, fortified with the new scenic methods, was developed in the other, indoor, playhouses. But needless to say, if we trace back from Restoration practices to the Globe, we shall miss altogether this medieval concomitant, which was so important a factor of its guise. The early restorers did not omit the medieval reference from their calculations, but they tended to give it a wrong emphasis; they allowed it to be a factor in the auditorium, but not much in the stagecraft: they allowed that it formed a part of the Elizabethan literary inheritance, but owing, perhaps, to their concentration on Shakespeare's work rather than on the great number of inferior plays which represent the more normal, run-of-the-mill tastes of the time, they assumed that it faded early from the scene, whereas it seems evident to many critics nowadays that it did not.

The practices of the modern stage are constant, almost universal. They work consistently within its accepted frame of scenic, lighting, orchestral and managerial arrangements, to such an extent that even the most rustic of amateur dramatic societies would consider itself naked and untutored if it could not provide itself with some sort of attempt at the curtain-and-lighting arrangements of a 'proper' theatre. But the Elizabethan company of players did not fashion its style upon the acceptance of any particular structure. The Chamberlain's Men at the Globe were well housed in their up-to-date building, but their plays and methods were such that they could be taken straight from there into the countryside, or into the Queen's banqueting hall, with hardly a change, in just the same way that Peter Quince and his men could first make 'this green plot . . . our stage, this hawthorn-brake our tiring house', and then go from there into the palace of Duke Theseus to give their performance. The character of the modern stage is rooted in the technical machinery that houses it and provides its effects. But the Elizabethan theatre was portable, self-contained, adjustable and independent of any surrounding other than its audience. The very stage itself needed to be no more than an open floor, which was only raised up for the better convenience of the spectators. And although we may find that the Elizabethans did make use in their fixed theatres of certain structural features which we interpret as having formed a part of their permanent stage building—e.g., an 'upper stage'—we ought not to suppose that every similar case refers of necessity to the same thing. We ought to leave space in our interpretations for variability and improvisation. The attempt to reconstruct Elizabethan theatres as though they were all permanently uniform, and a belief that the stage directions in plays, and some random textual references to stage conditions, all refer uniformly to certain permanent structural features which were to be found at all the theatres, surely ought not to be carried too far. It is a typically modern and 'technical' approach, of the kind which has in the past helped bring about some very dubious theories as to the whole nature of Elizabethan stagecraft. There was, for example, Carl Brodmeier's 'alternation' theory, now generally discredited. According to this the Elizabethans constructed their plays so as to allow the scenes to be acted alternately between the front and rear portions of the stage, which was divided, Brodmeier assumed, by a curtain suspended between the two great stage pillars. In this way the Elizabethans could be brought into line with the modern technique of changing the stage furniture and properties unseen behind curtains. Another more up-to-date and rather more complex theory assumes that the architecture of the Elizabethan stage was specially designed to allow for action to take place around a number of permanent structural units at different levels, such as on upper floors or at fixed doors and windows, and that plays were written with this complex stage in mind. Such methods, excellent to the modern mind, are not at all in the character of the Elizabethan one. Moreover, if such a theory as that last mentioned were true, it would imply that the Elizabethan actors had invented a form of stagecraft different from anything known before, which had no family connexion with any other theatrical style of its time, and which, in spite of its success in its own time, was eventually abandoned altogether. Such an isolated phenomenon would be unlikely in the world of the theatre at any time, and especially in the sixteenth century. Theatrical people have always been great respecters of traditional practices. Surely it would be far better to assume that the style of the Elizabethan theatre was based on tradition, and that it developed in accordance with the accepted theatrical modes of its day, not only the English mode, but that of the Netherlands, Germany, France and Italy also.

Here again the early critics were at a disadvantage, for there was little or no comparative theatrical history for them to draw upon. Before quite recent times the history of the theatre was confined (except for the memoirs of famous actors) to the history of dramatic *literature*, which is a rather different thing. All the ornate and gorgeous theatrical pomps of the Renaissance, all the popular jig-stuff, all the farces of the Italian Comedians, all the scenic ingenuities of Torelli, the Bibienas and Bérain, having no great literature to back them up, were considered to have no place for serious consideration. They existed only as drawings and engravings which most critics thought of as fantasies perhaps not seriously intended even for the stage. And for a long time there were no pictures at all of the interior of an Elizabethan theatre.

The nearest examples known were on the title pages of two Caroline-published plays, Alabaster's *Roxana* and Richards's *Messalina* (Plates 44 and 45), and these, apart from the fact that they each showed a prow-like stage backed by curtains, were not much help. Another picture, the frontispiece to Kirkman's *The Wits* (cf. page 39), showed the same kind of thing applying to a popular performance in Restoration times, evidently indoors; but this again was not much. Then in 1888 the German critic Karl Gaedertz published a drawing which he had found in the University Library of Utrecht. It showed an authentic view of the interior of the Swan theatre in London (Plate 7), which from associated evidence can be dated about the year 1596. The drawing tallies remarkably with the independent evidence of the old exterior views. It has the rounded house, the hut and the flag. It shows also that 'shadow or cover' over the stage, supported by posts, which are features mentioned in the Hope and Fortune contracts. But because it does not show a curtained recess at the rear of the stage, and is ambiguously if not badly drawn in other places, it has been sometimes criticised as an unsound foundation upon which to build. It is pointed out that it is only a report at second hand, being a copy by one man of an original sketch by another. Indeed, it may have been done only from a verbal description, with no previous drawing at all. But however that may be, one of the two men concerned in it had in fact visited London and had in fact seen the Swan theatre, and, as already noted, the evidence tallies with the other evidence we have. The drawing, then, whatever its faults and difficulties, must form, as Sir Edmund Chambers has said, 'the inevitable basis of any comprehensive account of the main structural features of a playhouse'. If we differ from it (as most reconstructions do, to some extent) it can only be either because we believe in the variability of the playhouses one from another, or else because we consider the picture faulty in some detail or other of draughtsmanship. But if evidence is to have any value at all we are not at liberty to differ from it very widely.

The publication of the Swan drawing enabled scholars to agree at last upon a general representative reconstruction of an Elizabethan playhouse, which, although still only conjectural, could be offered as a good basis for the understanding of Shakespearean production. All the evidence which had been so diligently assembled and studied for so long was now gathered in, so to speak, under the roof of the Swan and arranged to fit into the Swan framework. The result was a synthetic but very acceptable picture. In the following chapters of this book I propose to criticise it from certain angles, but with a view to adjusting it and perhaps adding to it here and there, if I can, and not with any idea of trying to disintegrate what has been so usefully put together. First, however, let us examine the picture as we find it, noting what features of it are certain, and what are conjectural.

It is certain, then, that the Elizabethan playgoer, when he approached one of the big public playhouses to see the afternoon's show, came in most cases to a round building (and I shall allow the word 'round' to include polygonal, since this gives the same general impression as opposed to a rectangular building). Built over the top of this round house was a hut, usually quite small (though in Hollar's engraving it is large), and over the hut there waved a flag. As he went in at the door he paid his money into a box, which was held by one of the playhouse staff called a 'gatherer'. This money allowed him to enter the open yard where stood the stage, and around the yard, overlooking the stage, three tiers of galleries were built up. (Three tiers are certain, at any rate, at the Fortune, the Hope and the Swan, which strongly indicate the same for the Globe and all the rest.) What we are not quite certain about is the arrangement of the main entrance doors. The Swan drawing shows none, and the inference is that it is placed centrally, facing the stage and below the station point from which the drawing purports to have been done. This is the supposition upon which all reconstructions are made, I think without exception. It is worth bearing in mind, however, that the first Globe had two doors. Sir Ralph Winwood, in a contemporary letter in which he referred to the burning-down of that building, remarked that 'it was a great marvaile . . . that the people had so little harm, having but two narrow doors to get out'. This is usually interpreted as referring to the public entrance on the one hand and the tiring-house or actors' entrance on the other. That interpretation may be right, but it is still worth questioning whether the letter-writer had not in his mind's eye the normal means of public access, which is what his words sound like, without thinking of the tiring-house door round at the back—if that is where it was. Besides, it is a most usual and commonsense axiom at public auditoriums that there must always be more doors for people to go out, which they do in a crowd at the end, than for their coming in, which they do in ones and twos at the beginning. If, then, the doors were narrow, as Sir Ralph Winwood says, it would be reasonable to assume that there were two *public doors*, one only being used for entrance, but both being flung open at the end of the show. And if there were two doors they would most likely have been placed not facing but flanking the stage and opposite to each other. In some of the black-and-white sketches in this book I have suggested this arrangement for what it is worth; and I think it is at least worth bearing in mind.

It appears that the entrances to the auditorium galleries led up out of the yard. At any rate, the Swan drawing seems to indicate this, and a scandalised person, writing in 1582,[1] declared that 'in the playhouses at London, it is the fashion of youthes to go first into the yarde, and there to carry their eye through every gallery' seeking for women to whom, when they see them, 'thither they flye, and presse as nere to ye fairest as they can'. He goes on to say that 'they give them pippines, they dally with their garments, to pass ye time'. However, it seems they got there by way of the yard, and it is known that in going from one part of the house to another they would be required to pay varying supplementary charges at the entrances to different divisions of the house. If they were poor they paid their penny for first entrance and went no farther than the yard, where they stood among the groundlings. If they were well-to-do and privileged they might take the 'Lord's room' or one of the 'gentleman's rooms' which are variously described as 'over' or 'next to' the stage. For a thorough analysis of the auditorium with its penny and two-penny galleries and its 'twelve-penny rooms', the reader is referred to John Cranford Adams's book *The Globe Playhouse*, though it should here be noted that Adams does not agree that the galleries were reached by way of the yard.

Now that he has entered and taken his place, the playgoer faces a stage which is familiar to him from whatever place or angle he may be viewing it; for he has often been here before, and the stage has always been the same. It is useful to remember this when considering the matter of the visibility of scenes on the Elizabethan stage. Their playhouses were not planned according to a scientific layout based on sight-lines as our modern theatres are, and visibility must have been bad from many parts of a house which was as prolific in posts and pillars as we know the Elizabethan playhouse to have been. But good visibility, essential in a modern theatre, which relies so much upon the effects of changeable scenery, is hardly of first importance, important though it may still be, in a theatre whose features are fixed, known and expected from one visit to the next.

The stage, as we know, was thrust out from one side of the surrounding house into the centre of the yard, like a great wooden peninsula. Of its shape, there is some question whether it was rectangular or tapering, but this and other matters concerned with the stage itself we are to discuss separately in Chapter 3. We shall also leave until later most of our consideration of the area around and within the house-wall at the back of the stage, the area called the tiring-house. Some points about it may be noted here, however. It is agreed

[1] Stephen Gosson, *Plays Confuted in Five Actions*, 1582.

in nearly all reconstructions that the interior of the tiring-house on the stage level was divided off from the stage by hangings of some sort, usually curtains opening in the middle. Contemporary texts sometimes mention curtains and sometimes arras, and it is worth while to note that the two are not the same in function: an arras is a fixed hanging, usually fairly heavy with painting, or a tapestry, which cannot be drawn aside like a curtain. Therefore if the opening at the rear of the stage should be hung with arras, one could make an entrance from it by lifting a flap of it at the sides or middle, but could not part it in such a way as to make the space behind it usable as a supplementary stage. But this could, of course, be done if the opening were hung with curtains, which could be drawn aside on rings. We will accept, then, for the time being, an opening at the back, which could be hung with either arras or curtains (although the Swan drawing does not show this). We will accept also the convention that on each side of this opening were two doors, such as are shown in the Swan drawing. We will agree that these doors may have been a part of Elizabethan stage practice which was carried over to later times, and that these doors were the prototypes of the famous apron-stage doors of the Restoration theatres; but we should note in passing that the convention which allows us to imagine only a single pair of stage doors for every type of Elizabethan stage has to reckon with a certain number of contradictory stage directions like 'Enter three in black clokes, at three doores', from the *Four Prentices of London*. Perhaps there was a third door at the back within the opening, which is the solution usually given; but one would be at liberty, so far as hard evidence is concerned, to make a reconstruction envisaging three or more doors if one wished to do so. Neither, of necessity, need such doors be large. There is an argument that they would have to be large enough to allow the entrance of spectacular processional objects such as Tamburlaine's chariot and the cage of Bajazet, in Marlowe's *Tamburlaine*. But it is equally if not more likely that such things would be brought in through the central hangings, when there were any, as they are through the hangings at the ring entrance of any travelling circus to-day. Of course, the Swan drawing does show large doors; but in this case there are no hangings.

So much for the time being about the features of the stage rear wall. Let us now turn back to the stage itself, to consider the two great posts which stood upon it. These are among our unquestionable facts, and for most people they represent more than any other thing the typical and curious nature of the Elizabethan stage. Visibility once again comes into question. How could such a pair of pillars be so placed as they are shown to be in the Swan drawing and not impair visibility, especially of anything taking place on the rear part of the stage? The answer must be that the pillars *did* impair visibility; and that was that. To what extent they did so would depend upon their exact placing and upon the amount of use made of the rear parts of the stage (I think myself that modern commentators have tended to put far too much stress upon this area at the back, and that the general tendency was for the actors to come right out into the forward parts, near to the most central point of the surrounding audience). But there the pillars stood, and it is generally agreed that the actors sometimes made use of them, as is found in Haughton's *Englishmen for my Money*, where two characters, supposed to be groping their way along in the dark, bump into them one after the other, and presently declare them to be a couple of may-poles. Most commentators seem to think that these pillars were conventionally used to represent trees, and that when characters were supposed to climb a tree, as in Jonson's *The Case is Altered*, IV, iv, where a stage direction says that the character Onion does so, they somehow climbed up this pillar, or some part of it, such as on to the plinth. It is also supposed that the cutpurses whom 'we tye to a poast on our stage, for all people to wonder at, when at a play they are taken pilfring'[1] were tied to one of these. I cannot agree with either of these assumptions. There is no way of climbing these pillars that could be either convenient or effective. It is far more reasonable to suppose that these cases refer to the use of other smaller posts, probably at the rear of the stage against the tiring-house, where a character could climb up into a 'tree' at the first gallery level. Any sort of elaboration of the tiring-house façade in the Elizabethan style is likely to have produced ornamental pillars, and we know that at the Hope, where there were definitely no pillars at all supporting the roof-canopy over the stage (which was the function of those at the Swan) there were none the less some 'turned columns upon and over the stage'. The meaning of this is not clear, but in its context it seems to me to indicate pillars against the tiring-house façade.

The roof-canopy referred to above was that part of the area overhanging the stage which was generally called the Heavens, and which the Fortune contract calls the 'shadow or cover'. The function of that forward pent-roof over half the stage in the Swan drawing must have been to give partial shelter in unsettled weather, to prevent a play being interrupted by a short shower of rain. (On really wet days, of course, there would be no performances.) But the hut which stood, so typical a feature, up above all the rest of the theatre, was clearly the place where was housed the hoisting machinery which

[1] William Kemp, *Nine Days' Wonder*.

raised and lowered the cloud-wreathed thrones and chariots of gods and magicians between the Heavens and the stage. Seen from below, the underside of the hut and of the 'shadow' roof, would have presented a fine spectacle of ornamental painting. It has been pointed out by T. S. Graves [1] that there are many references in plays of the period which suggest there was some sort of ornamental zodiac motif painted in the upper regions over the stage. This has been generally accepted, and in his *From Art to Theatre*, p. 96, G. R. Kernodle reproduces a picture of a sixteenth-century ceiling painted in just this way. In the midst of the painted ceiling there was a trapdoor through which, when opened, the 'creaking throne comes down, the boyes to please', as Ben Jonson described it in the Prologue to *Every Man In His Humour*. The creaking, if there was any (for Jonson may have written more in detraction than in truth: he did not care for this style of play) would have been disguised as far as possible by music or by thunder—for also in the hut was the cannon-ball which was rumbled down the thunder-run for this purpose. The effect was also produced from up there by beating a drum. Lightning, shooting stars and similar effects were contrived probably by means of fireworks running down from the Heavens on a fixed wire.

But the Heavens need not have referred only to the hut and the roof. It is likely that there was some upper gallery, which cannot be seen in the Swan drawing because of the angle from which the sketch has been made, which also could have formed a part of the Heavens feature. Most commentators now agree on this. The only difficulty it raises is that of the actual height of the shadow-roof above the stage. The present tendency is to conclude that the underside of the roof would have been on a level with the eaves of the theatre building. This would allow better visibility of the stage from the top gallery of the auditorium, which, if the 'shadow' jutted forward from *below* the eaves level, as is shown in the Swan drawing, would have provided a rather impaired view on this account. However, if the 'shadow' were to be raised high up to the eaves-line, it would necessitate elongating, in what I think is a most improbable way, the two pillars supporting it in front. Clearly the two pillars in the Swan sketch are intended to be in the classical style and proportion. But to raise them in anything like classical proportion to the height of approximately thirty feet (which is what would be required) would be to make them unwieldily massive for their job. On the other hand, to make them of that height but slender, would be to add structural difficulties to architectural improbabilities; for two such tall, slender single-piece shafts of timber would

[1] T. S. Graves, *The Court and the London Theatres during the Reign of Elizabeth*, 1913.

not only be unsuitable for carrying a permanent weight but, moreover, would not be easy to get. And even if, as Adams suggests, ships' masts could be satisfactorily used for the job, the result would still have been so out of character with the Elizabethan style and method of building that I, for one, think it more likely the pillars were kept pretty well within the classical proportion, that they therefore did not rise to the eaves-line, and that people in the top galleries whose view was consequently impaired by the 'shadow', were obliged to make the best of it, as we have to do to-day in some of the upper galleries of our own theatres.

In spite of this, however, there is no reason to disbelieve in the existence of a third storey in the tiring-house façade, and if it existed it would probably have embraced a part of the function of the Heavens. The zodiacal signs and stars that were painted upon the ceiling could also have surrounded this. There is in Webster's *The White Devil*, V, iv, a scene where Flamineo is confronted by a ghost. Flamineo outfaces it, speaks boldly to it, asks where it comes from, whether from Heaven or Hell. The words had their familiar theatrical connotation. Hell was the place beneath the stage, out of which ghosts, devils and infernal visions were wont to rise up through a trapdoor. It was the 'cellarage' in which the voice of Hamlet's dead father was heard. And Heaven as we have seen was the region over the top of the stage. So Flamineo puts his question to the ghost in a theatrical metaphor: 'In what place art thou?' he asks, 'in yon starry gallery, or in the cursed dungeon?'

From this we may assume there was a 'starry gallery' somewhere aloft, and it is reasonable to suppose it was in a third storey of the tiring-house façade. In my reconstruction sketch based on the Swan drawing (page 174) I have contrived to keep a foot in both camps. I have kept the stage posts to a reasonable height (about 22 feet), have brought the shadow down accordingly, and have tucked the starry gallery up inside it.

G. R. Kernodle considers that not all the scenes in which the gods appear on thrones in Elizabethan plays refer necessarily to the 'creaking' throne which descended, 'the boyes to please'. He quotes the displays of 'Thrones of Honour' used on occasions of royal or scholastic ceremonial to show how a god-like or allegorical tableau could be set high up in an ornamental façade. (Examples of this effect can be seen in Plate 30, where Peace sits throned aloft with War grovelling at her feet, or in Plate 32, where Peace and Plenty sit together presiding from their high throne over the Garden of Plenty.) John Cranford Adams considers that in *The Tempest*, III, iii, this high gallery was 'the top' where Prospero stood, invisible, to direct his Spirits at the magic banquet. But was this also 'the top' upon which Joan La Pucelle appeared in 1 *Henry VI*, III, ii, 'thrusting out a torch burning' to signal to her allies the way into the besieged town of Rouen? Both John C. Adams and Sir Edmund Chambers agree that it was. My only demur on the point is that the whole of the warfare which flounces back and forth and around the stage in this play is of such a pasteboard-and-trumpet kind that I cannot help but think the towns of Orleans and Rouen were in keeping, and may well have been represented in the simple terms of the *Laurentius* stage in Cologne (Plate 15). But that argument raises a subject beyond the proper scope of this chapter, though it is one to which I shall return later.

3. The Unworthy Scaffold

IN MOST of the attempts that have been made during the last fifty years to establish a convincing reconstruction of the Elizabethan public playhouse, the main force of controversy has nearly always raged around that area at the back of the stage which is sometimes called the 'tiring-house façade'. In their various assessments of this feature most reconstructions disagree with one another; yet while students have been so earnestly concentrating upon this area of disagreement, they have accepted without much question a number of preconceived opinions about the nature of the great acting area, the stage itself. In estimating the character of the Elizabethan theatre we are constantly being betrayed by the habits of our modern theatrical experience. We try, seemingly in spite of our better knowledge, to find some sort of a proscenium somewhere upon the Elizabethan stage; to open up an inner stage, no matter how questionable the evidence for its existence, and to thrust back into it a greater and greater portion of the action of the Elizabethan plays. In this way the tiring-house façade has seemed, like a magnet, to draw back both actors and students alike into itself, leaving the great stage before it empty and unattended. But let us change our point of

34

view for a while; let us turn our backs upon the tiring-house, leaving its problems and disagreements unresolved, and inspect some details of that feature which Shakespeare, in the Prologue to *Henry V*, called an 'unworthy scaffold'—the stage itself. There is reason to suppose that we have misinterpreted some of its features, which, if we can come to see them more clearly, may assist us when we return again to examine the tiring-house.

We cannot begin better than by re-examining the Swan drawing. We must try to bring to this not only the knowledge gained from all the research into theatrical history that has taken place since it was first discovered, but also, if we can, a 'fresh eye', as painters say, with which to try and see it as though for the first time. Looked at in this way it may seem to us that one of its most remarkable features is also one which has been so long accepted for a commonplace that it now passes as a thing not worth further inquiry. This is none other than that the drawing shows a large rectangular stage set out into a round arena, a square peg in a round hole. If we could come fresh to this arrangement, surely it would strike us at once as a rather clumsy and uncomfortable feature. Those two wedge-like spaces upon either side of the stage, how awkward they are, how offensive to the general sense of architectural fitness! One asks oneself, why did not the builders of the Swan carry the stage right across from one side of the yard to the other? What is the purpose of those wedges? To accommodate the 'groundling' spectators in the yard? One supposes so, disregarding for the moment the familiar dandies sitting on the stage, who, by all logical analysis, would be sitting just here along the sides, in the way of just those very groundlings. Surely this cannot have been a very advantageous place for groundlings to stand? Or let us look at this same feature at the Fortune. This, it will be recalled, was a square playhouse; here at least the square peg was fitted in a square hole, and, since we have the builder's contract for it, we can expect some very precise information as to how it was done. And yet here again the effect is most surprising. Here, by any logical interpretation of the contract, there is a space of ground running along each side of the stage between the stage and its neighbouring galleries, which, while it measured only 6 feet wide from stage to gallery, was no less than $27\frac{1}{2}$ feet long. In other words, these two spaces, one on each side of the stage, have the dimensions of corridors or gangways rather than of convenient parts of the auditorium: and when we consider, as we shall do shortly, that the Elizabethan stage was probably built up much higher than modern stages are, so that spectators, to get a comfortable view, would be apt to stand a little way off, not close up against it, we are led again to think that whatever their uses may have been, these spaces at the sides of the Fortune stage could hardly have been *designed* for the comfort and convenience of spectators.

The general feeling that these stage-side spaces are a piece of awkwardness is reflected in the readiness of scholars to abandon them as untrue. On the face of it, it would seem to make a much better general design, as well for the round playhouses of the Bankside as for the square Fortune, if these stages were to taper, narrowing towards the front, thus opening out the side spaces and allowing better movement and more room for spectators in the yard. The *Roxana* and *Messalina* engravings appear to give some countenance to this notion, which has been adopted in a number of important reconstructions, the two most notable being Albright's in 1909, and J. Cranford Adams's in 1943. But still it will not do: it is not convincing enough. The combined evidence of the de Witt sketch and the Fortune contract alone, without counting any lesser arguments and deductions, is very strong, and the value of *Roxana* and *Messalina* is too unsure. We do not know what sort of stages, whether indoor or outdoor, permanent or temporary, public or private, these are meant to represent. We only know that in spite of their particular convenience in some respects, they are not typical of stages of the period as a whole. When the balance of the evidence is made and all the likelihoods assessed, one is left with the probability that the typical Elizabethan stage was rectangular, just as the Swan drawing shows it. In other words, we are left with an architectural design which, when set inside a round auditorium, we do not like very much, which we feel to be unsatisfactory, requiring some further explanation. It is a problem; and to attempt to alter it, to rectify the design to suit ourselves; to assume, for example, that the Swan drawing is inaccurate, and that it ought to have shown a tapering stage like the *Roxana* and *Messalina* ones; to assume such things as this simply to bring the drawing into line with our own ideas of architectural fitness is to shirk the problem at just that point where, if we pursue it, if we press it hard just where it appears so clumsy and inexplicable, we may prove to have hit upon the very root and spring of the matter, which will there open up and reveal its explanation. For instance, the word 'design' has been used above: it was said that we feel something unsatisfactory about the *design* of the stage . . .; and here we should pause, for surely in the modern sense there was no such thing as a *design* for an Elizabethan stage, nor yet for the playhouse it stood in. We have been betrayed by our modern approach. We should know well enough that these places were not designed on drawing-boards as they would be to-day, but erected according to rule of thumb and traditional methods by master masons and their craftsmen. We are not concerned here with designs, but with traditions. Is it not possible, therefore, that both the stage and the house it stood in were *traditional* in form, and that the only innovation made by James Burbage, when he erected the first public playhouse, The Theatre, in 1575, was to make a rough-and-ready combination of the two?

It has grown to be commonly accepted that the Elizabethan playhouse derived its form from that of the galleried inn-yards in which, in earlier days,

Early amphitheatres on Bankside
(From Ralph Agas' map of London, published between 1560 and 1590)

the old stages were set up; and that the stage itself, being then an improvised affair, adopted certain of the features, doors, windows, galleries and so on, which were found most useful and usual at those inns. This theory, for which there is no authentic evidence at all, has been given more credit than it deserves. Certainly it was common at one time for plays to be performed in inn-yards, but more than this we do not know, and we are not justified in assuming that the inn-yard gave any other feature to the theatres than the convenience of the use of galleries; a feature which could in any case have been seen already in use at the bull- and bear-baiting arenas on Bankside, years before the first theatres were built. In any case the first theatres, as is

generally agreed, were round or polygonal buildings, which does not argue
very strongly for their resemblance to the yards of any known kind of inn.
Surely the most apt question is: *what sort of a stage in fact was it that was set
up, in the early days, in those inn-yards*? Are we perhaps justified in supposing that it was some traditional form of stage which was later transferred,
perhaps with a few modifications, but substantially the same, to the round-
shaped Theatre, then to the Curtain, and to all the other playhouses, of whatever shape, round, polygonal or square, modifying, enlarging, aggrandising
itself perhaps in one way or another, but always remaining within touch of a
tradition whose conventions were fixed long before Burbage was a baby?
There are things which lend some colour to this possibility. For instance, the
Fortune builder's contract provides that this theatre shall be fitted with a stage
'contryved and fashioned like unto the Stadge of the saide Plaie howse called
the Globe'. It seems to have bothered no one that the Globe was a round or
polygonal building, while the Fortune was square. Evidently the character of
the stage derived nothing from the roundness of the one nor the squareness
of the other, but had its own nature to keep to, and kept to it, no matter
what the shape of its surroundings. Even when an improvised stage was set
up indoors, where one might expect to find that it was built right across one
end of a hall or room, one finds, instead, a stage built out from one wall into
the middle of the room, just as the Swan stage was built out into the middle of
the yard. Such at least is the stage we see in the well-known frontispiece to
Kirkman's *The Wits; or Sport Upon Sport*. It must surely be that one of the
factors, probably the chief factor, maybe even the only factor which made
this stage this shape, was the very strong factor of an abiding tradition.

Besides this it may be noted that contemporary visitors to the London
playhouses appear to have been very impressed by them; but not for the
technical reasons by which, if they had vouchsafed them, their descriptions
could have been so useful to us to-day. What impressed them was simply
the then very unusual business of providing a large, permanent, public
auditorium; of the stages, and how plays were performed on them, and, for
instance, whether there was such a thing as an inner stage or not, they have
nothing whatever to say. One is tempted to think that in this regard they
found nothing essentially different from traditional practices they had seen
elsewhere, even in other countries, and so did not bother to report upon them.

The inferences, slender though they may seem, are worth pursuing, because
we can at once point to the existence, in full flourish, of a traditional stage
of the very type we are seeking. It is none other than the old street theatre,

Frontispiece to *The Wits; or Sport Upon Sport*
by Francis Kirkman, 1672

the booth stage of the market-place, the *théâtre de foire*. This is perhaps most familiar to us in engravings of seventeenth- and eighteenth-century strolling players, especially of the Commedia dell' Arte. But its lineage, as Richard Southern has pointed out in his study of the subject,[1] is much older than that, and its descendants more recent. Its earliest portraits are found in Greek vase-paintings of phlyax comedies, while some photographs taken a few years ago at Tardets, in the Pyrenees (Plate 22), show Basque peasants dancing their traditional folk dances on this same traditional stage. Its form does not vary much between one century and another. Basically it consists of no more than a platform supported on posts or trestles, behind which is some sort of small house or tent from which the actors come out. Here we may recognise, if we will, an early form of the Elizabethan tiring-house. The picture of this basic stage given on page 51 is general rather than particular: it purports to show a typical structure of which all the specific instances of which we have record are variations in one degree or another. Sometimes, as shown in the English engraved title-page to Scarron's *Comical Romance*, of the Restoration period (Plate 23), we see it in its simplest manner, though with some small additions it can quickly take on the more ornamental appearance of the Lyons *Terence* stages of the fifteenth century; or, elaborated almost out of recognition, but still fundamentally the same thing, it can present us with those baroque towers and arcades of the Flemish Rederyker stages of the sixteenth century, which may be studied in George R. Kernodle's book, *From Art to Theatre*. Here again we are on the threshold of the Elizabethan playhouse, as Kernodle shows.

There are two special characteristics of this traditional street theatre, which

[1] In Chapter I of his book *The Open Stage* Southern writes as follows:

'I once made an attempt . . . to represent in a chart the development of stage and theatre structure throughout Europe after the fashion of a genealogical tree, wherein the Hellenistic stage descended from the classical Greek stage and then led to the Graeco-Roman and the Roman, and where the mansion-stage of the Middle Ages led to the simultaneous settings of the 16th-century Terentian stages and thence to Mahelot's scenes at the Hôtel de Bourgogne—and so forth; a somewhat artificial attempt that presented me with numerous breaks and failed to be consistently convincing—except on one notable point: one thing did stand out; one form of stage could be traced at any period and reasonably shown to have an unbroken development, though it was

so simple and so adequate for its purpose that it betrayed few signs of the changes of evolution. It was the little strolling-players' stage which is much the same on the Greek mime vases, in the simpler mediaeval fit-ups, in the quack-doctor, or mountebank stages, the simpler Commedia dell' Arte platforms, the booths of the Victorian fairs, some of the penny gaffs, and the pierrots' home on the sands at any seaside resort today.

'It was, briefly, a fairly high platform with some sort of booth at the back from which the players came, and with possibly a canopy above, but otherwise generally innocent of further elaboration. It is because of this players' room behind that I name the type the "booth" stage.'

I am much indebted to Southern for this analysis, which became the germ of the theory I am presenting in this chapter.

recur so frequently in pictures of it as to deserve our special attention. One is, that it seems not to have had any fundamental qualms about revealing the naked trestles that supported its stage. True, these were often hidden behind draperies; but when, as often happened, they were allowed to show, this would seem not to have been necessarily from lack of means (for in the Lyons woodcuts illustrating Terence's *Andria*, which show a pleasantly ornamented stage façade, not lacking for the necessary decorative skill or expense, we find at the same time that the naked timbers beneath the stage are plainly represented), but simply, we must suppose, because an audience was willing, at need, to accept the convention of turning a blind eye upon things which did not come within the action of the play. When Shakespeare called his stage an 'unworthy scaffold' he was not using the word scaffold in any metaphorical sense. It was in his day an ordinary synonym for stage. A stage was simply a scaffold for actors, differing little from that other scaffold upon which, perhaps in the selfsame market-place, the public executioner performed his own mystery; and in both cases the scaffolding itself might be either draped or left bare as occasion dictated; and in neither case did it matter much, so long as the performers were raised up high enough for all the crowd to see them.

This brings us to the second characteristic feature we are to notice as having been typical of the street theatres; this is the unusual height of the stage, as compared with our modern custom. It varied, of course, and not every contemporary picture will support the claim; but the evidence is good and plentiful enough to show that the stage-floor of a typical street theatre was set level with the tops of the heads of the spectators standing around it, if not a little higher (Plate 16). The reason for this is obvious. The shows were meant to be seen by large crowds standing on flat ground, and if the people at the back were to be able to see, then the spectacle had to be raised up high enough for them to do so: the only alternative would have been to have the spectators themselves raised on stands, or on a raked floor, which was here out of the question. This, as we know, was the case with the medieval street-shows, where the stages, either static or on waggons, were frequently set high enough to allow for a dressing-room underneath. One of the best pictures we have of the pageant cars of the old medieval tradition is 'The Triumph of Isabella', an early seventeenth-century Flemish painting now in the Victoria and Albert Museum. Two extracts from this are shown in Plates 24 and 25. The whole painting shows a procession of ten splendid cars, part of the celebrations in honour of the Archduchess Isabella of the Netherlands in 1615. The picture is skilfully and realistically painted, and from it we can judge that the floor-level of the various cars was set at about 5 feet 6 inches above the ground. Another picture, van der Meulen's painting in the Liechtenstein Gallery, Vienna,[1] of a stage set up in a market-place, a very circumstantial and fully detailed record dating from the 1660s, gives a similar result—though here 5 feet 6 inches would appear to be the minimum height, and one might even put it a little higher. Several other pictures revealing this habit for stages to be high can be found among the Plates at the end of this book. In general, a reasonable guess would put the normal stage height for a street theatre playing to standing spectators as somewhere between 5 feet 6 inches and 6 feet above the ground.

These, then, are some of the characteristics of a traditional stage which I here suggest was the immediate parent of the Elizabethan one. We can imagine it, quite small at first, being erected in the yards of the London inns; then having room to expand in Burbage's newly built arena, enlarging itself, and that little tabernacle at the back, the rudimentary tiring-house, enlarging itself also, adding an upper storey or even two, incorporating itself into the structure of the main building, and presently, with the further addition of a canopied Heavens, becoming the façade we know—or think we know. We must recall, however, that this is not the course of development that has hitherto been supposed; the usual theory is that the features of the tiring-house were originally adapted from the existing gallery framework of the auditorium, and its general design was fundamentally conditioned by this framework. But it must be remembered that this is no more than a conjecture; there is no special evidence for it; and although the theory here offered as an alternative is also conjecture, there are a few indications of something which, if they are not evidence to support it, at least nod in that direction. For instance, it will be remembered that in the Fortune contract the builder is first given his instructions for building the playhouse 'frame', i.e., the general structure of the auditorium, and is then given further directions for a 'Stadge and Tyreinge howse to be made, erected & sett upp *within* the saide fframe'. The italics are mine, and I emphasise the word because it seems to indicate that not only the stage but the tiring-house also was thought of as a separate structure. Furthermore, it is quite clear in the Swan drawing that the tiring-house façade is flat and that it stands forward and apart from the round structure of the auditorium, in which it may be incorporated, but of which it is *not* an essential member.

[1] Reproduced in James Laver, *Drama*, p. 122.

However, it is not with the tiring-house but with the stage that we are at present concerned. We will assume, at least for the time being, that this theory as to the origin of the Elizabethan stage structure is correct. Approaching it from this angle, let us see what new light is thrown upon the business of reconstruction. First, let us go back to the street theatre where we left it just now, considering the height of the stage.

If it is agreed that in the period we are studying an outdoor stage for a standing audience would tend to be a high one, about on a level with the top of a man's head, may we not assume that this characteristic was continued in at least some of the Shakespearean playhouses? There is a strong argument for this. We know that an indispensable feature of these theatres was the space under the stage called the Hell, and to allow for this most, if not all, reconstructions hitherto (which provide for a stage between 4 and 5 feet high, and no higher) have had recourse to an excavated cellar beneath the stage, to give the necessary headroom. This immediately raises a problem, for the evidence of the Hope Theatre is certainly against it; here, we are told, the stage was made 'to be carryed or taken awaie, and to stande uppon tressels', so that when desired the arena could be left free for 'the game of Beares and Bulls to be bayted in the same': which means that in this case a dug cellar cannot be considered as at all probable. But in any case, to have gone digging cellars on the Bankside of Shakespeare's day was to go digging for trouble. Whenever the Thames was at high tide this locality was then little better than a marsh, and the rising water was collected in ponds and ditches which, as the tide went down, discharged it again into the river. The Globe Playhouse itself was, as Ben Jonson tells us, built upon piles, 'Flancked with a ditch, and forc'd out of a Marish'. We can imagine, if we must, that the builders, being determined to provide Burbage with a cellar, may have dug down 1 foot or, with some ingenuity and a good deal of pumping, 2 feet. Deeper is unlikely: and in view of what we have seen at the Hope, and of what we have seen of the street theatres, is it not more likely that they dug no cellar at all, left their yard flat, and built their stage up, like other stages, high?

In a speculation like this where exact evidence is all too rare, we are often obliged, for want of better, to accept the most reasonable probability: which is in this case that a typical Elizabethan public theatre stage was apt to be much higher than we have formerly imagined, and that the activities of the Hell took place on a level with the groundling spectators around it, in the same way that it had always been done in medieval times. The actor had the heads of his groundlings not at his knees but at his feet, and Ben Jonson's pun about the '*understanding* gentlemen o' the ground' gains point when we see his speaker standing so high above them.

Turning now to the actual structure of these stages, we find that we have evidence of four of them, and that these are all different. In three of these cases the evidence is direct; in the fourth, the Globe, it is inferred.

First is the Swan, and our evidence is, of course, the drawing. It appears clear enough to be acceptable that the draughtsman intended to present what we will call an open stage, that is a stage left open beneath, so as to reveal its supports. We have already seen that this was not an unusual feature in the street theatres, and so its presence here at the Swan is no freak, but a direct link with tradition. We wish, however, that we could make more sense out of those two great baulks with which the front of the stage appears to be supported. Presumably there were two others farther back, beneath the two pillars supporting the Heavens, where they would certainly have been needed. A reconstruction along these lines would make sense, except that some sort of modification would be needed to provide support for the two forward corners of the stage. But these are details which tend to take us beyond the thread of our present study. Having found at the Swan some evidence for an open stage, we will pass on to the Fortune, where we can be certain of the opposite.

From the builder's contract we learn that the Fortune stage measured no less than 43 by 27½ feet, and since no other reference is given we must understand it to have been rectangular in plan. Its height above ground is not specified. However, we are told that it is to be 'paled in belowe with good stronge and sufficyent newe oken bourdes . . .', and soon after there follows a further detail about this, which seems hitherto to have been misunderstood, judging from previous reconstructions based upon the contract. The passage in question provides that 'all the princypall and maine postes of the saide fframe [i.e., of the house] and Stadge forwarde shalbe square and wroughte palaster-wise with carved proporcions called Satiers to be placed & sett on the topp of every of the same postes . . .' From this it must be assumed that the stage was all supported underneath with posts, of which those on the outer or 'forwarde' side were to be cut square, ornamented at the tops with the famous carved Satiers, and set 'palasterwise' against the paling of oaken boards previously referred to. The effect thus produced is shown in the drawing at the opening of Chapter 2 (and it may be noticed in passing that it is very like the front of the stage in the well-known woodcut from Parabosco's *Il Pellegrino*). The significance of this is that the stage is *seen* to be carried on posts in the traditional manner. The paling appears only as a sort of curtain wall between the posts.

As was said above, however, other reconstructions have interpreted this passage differently. In these the 'princypall and maine postes of the . . . Stadge forwarde' have been judged to belong not to the stage proper but to the tiring-house façade, and there, 'palasterwise', some posts have been duly arranged. The point is important to us here, and in a further instance which will arise later, because it involves our interpretation of the word 'stage' as the Elizabethans understood it. In the modern sense it is an elastic word involving not only the boards and timbers of the stage itself, but, if need be, the whole area in which it is set, the atmosphere with which it is invested, and indeed the very profession of those who act upon it. Not so to the Elizabethans. To them a stage was a scaffold, a raised floor, and no more; and we ought not to interpret their use of the word in any wider sense. The tiring-house was an adjacent but separate thing, and did not come within the meaning of the word stage.[1]

With all this in mind we will look at those parts of the Fortune contract which refer to the stage of the Globe. It will be remembered that the Fortune was built to rival the Globe, and the builder was directed to copy many of its arrangements. Certain differences are particularised, however. For instance, after the clause where it says that the Fortune stage was to be paled in below with oaken boards, it then goes on to say that it was to be 'in all *other* proporcions . . . contryved and fashioned like unto the Stadge of the saide Plaie howse called the Globe'. The word 'other' seems to imply the possibility that at the Globe the stage was *not* boarded in below, an implication which is later reinforced in a passage (already partly quoted above) which goes like this: 'To be made & doen to be in all other contrivitions, conveyances, fashions, thinge and thinges effected, finished and doen according to the manner and fashion of the said howse called the Globe *saveinge only* that all the princypall and maine postes of the saide fframe and Stadge forwarde shalbe square and wroughte palasterwise . . .'. In other words, the principal

---

[1] It is similarly interesting to note that our modern habit of referring to the Elizabethan form of stage as a 'platform stage' is equally out of keeping with their usage. For the Elizabethans the word platform meant a ground-plan, a levelled foundation, or even simply a design or policy, as we still do when we speak of a 'political platform'. A 'platform stage' would have been for an Elizabethan almost a contradiction in terms, and ones does not find them using the expression. In Thomas Platter's account of his visit to a London playhouse in 1599 there is a sentence which Chambers (*Elizabethan Stage*, ii, 365) has translated as 'they play on a raised platform, and everyone can well see it all'. But Platter's actual words in the German are 'erhöchten brüge', which I take to mean a 'high-standing bridge'.

and main posts of the stage at the Globe were *not* square as they were at the Fortune; therefore presumably they were round. And they were not set pilasterwise, as indeed, not being square, how could they have been? How, then, was the stage boarded in below? There are two possibilities: either the boards were set fully behind the outer posts in such a way as to leave them standing free, or else they were set fully in front of them, to make a continuous panelling in which the posts did not feature. Either is possible; but neither seems to be quite in tune with the likely practice of an Elizabethan

A stage supported on posts
Woodcut from Parabosco's *Il Pellegrino*, 1552

joiner. At any rate we ought to consider a third possibility, which is that the stage was not boarded in at all, but was left open. 'They might distinctly perceive a goodly stage to be reared (shining to sight like the bright burnished gold) upon many a fair pillar of clearest crystal.' The passage in the *English Wagner Book* of 1594, from which that sentence is taken, is quoted by Chambers as aptly reflecting—though in glorified terms—the general effect of the Elizabethan public stage, and it begins by emphasising those ranks of supporting pillars which, we suggest (allowing for some poetic licence in the matter of the clearest crystal), were a well-known stage feature.

And not only pillars but trestles. The last of the four stages in our evidence is that of the Hope, which as we have already noticed, was made to stand upon trestles 'to be carried or taken away'. Here, if the stage was boarded in, there is nothing in the Hope contract to suggest it; the general structure of trestles does not offer any very suitable way of doing it; and the character of the thing, from a traditional point of view, is entirely against it. Probability here again inclines on the side of the open stage.

Thus of our four stages only one is known for certain to have been paled in. With each of the others there is some reason to believe that the structure was an open one of posts or trestles, not concealed behind boards. But this is not to say that the structure was therefore left naked. Although we believe that in the street theatres this was sometimes done, and although we have the immediate evidence of the Swan drawing to the same effect, there is also some evidence which tells us that this was not the usual course. The stage was closed in below, not with boards but with hangings. This had been a practice with the street and booth stages from the very beginning, and its vestiges are hanging upon every Punch and Judy show to this day. For Elizabethan times, there is quite a deal of familiar textual evidence which will back up a theory that the Fortune stage, in being panelled, was not typical, but an innovation. The evidence for hangings has been misunderstood because, as stated above, scholars have allowed themselves to believe that the word 'stage' could be read as applying to the façade of the tiring-house. Thus when (in *Lucrece* 766) Shakespeare gives us:

> Black stage for tragedies and murthers fell

we have been told that he meant not that the stage, the scaffold, was all hung round with black, like the scaffold for a public execution, but that some black draperies were used behind or over the stage. Indeed, this may also have been done, but first Shakespeare tells us that it was the *stage*, not the tiring-house, which was black. Again, in the Induction to the anonymous play *A Warning or Fair Women* we have the lines:

> The stage is hung with black, and I perceive
> The auditors prepar'd for tragedie.

Or there is the quotation from Sidney's *Arcadia*, describing the clouds coming over the sun, which 'blacked over all the face of heaven; preparing (as it were) a mournful stage for a Tragedie to be played on'. Note that the Tragedy is played *on* the black and mournful stage, not 'within' or 'before' it. But if none of this is unambiguous enough, the following from Heywood's *Apology for Actors* leaves no doubt as to where the hangings were placed. He is speaking in the person of Melpomene and is purporting to describe the theatre of ancient time. His terms, however, as G. R. Kernodle says, are altogether those of a glorified Elizabethan stage, and in one sentence he refers to the matter of stage-hangings: 'Then did I tread on arras, cloth of tissue *hung round the fore-front of my stage.*' Taken in conjunction with what we know of medieval practice, of the street theatres, of the stage-structures at the Swan and the Hope, and even possibly at the Globe, and remembering that Heywood's own theatrical connexion was with the Red Bull, so that he may have had that theatre most in mind when he wrote the passage given above, are we not justified in supposing that if there was ever such a thing as a 'typical' Elizabethan stage, we ought to imagine it as being hung all round with a great skirt of cloth, perhaps one of several sets of hangings of different colours suitable to different types of play, hangings which had been much used and rough-handled like the shabby splendours of some travelling circus to-day, and which sometimes hung loose so that the draughts would stir its fringes a little in the dust, or maybe sometimes were lashed tight from post to post, to keep the groundlings from peering in too much at the preparations being made for them in Hell?

Or sometimes these hangings would be pulled aside, and the occupants of Hell could run out with fireworks into the middle of the crowd. There is an episode in *The Plot of the Play called England's Joy* which demonstrates this. The Plot, which, is the only surviving example of an Elizabethan playbill, gives the outline of a spectacular play dealing, in the manner of an allegory, with the glorious victories of Elizabeth. It is entirely reminiscent of those animated triumphal arches and *tableaux vivants* erected for the state entry of James I into London, of the royal entertainments at Kenilworth and Elvetham, and of the mode of the Flemish Rederyker shows; and in keeping with all this it ends with an apotheosis and the display of a Throne of Honour. The Heavenly spectacle is then at once contrasted with a Hellish one. The whole sequence reads:

. . . And so with music both with voice and instruments she is taken up into Heaven, when presently appears a Throne of blessed souls, and beneath *under the stage* set forth with strange fireworks, divers black and damned souls, wonderfully described in their several torments.

Now it can be objected that *England's Joy* is not in the first class of evidence, since so far as we know the play never existed. The existing Plot of it refers only to the hoax of March 1602, when one Richard Venner, having beguiled a large audience to the Swan to see this fabulous production, produced nothing, and welshed with the gate-money. The Plot is a dud prospectus; but as such it must needs have been written to be convincing to its readers, which it would not have been if it had promised an entertainment which, in the ordinary citizen's view, could not have been accomplished at the Swan. Besides, nothing in the whole document is foreign to what we already know of Elizabethan theatrical practice except this last item of a tableau presented under the stage. But may we not accept this also? It is already corroborated for us by de Witt that the Swan had an open stage. Thus the tableau described would have been presented between those two great supports shown in the drawing, and would, surely, have been revealed when the time came by drawing aside the stage-hangings.

But what of the visibility of this, when there was a mob of groundlings to shut out the sight of it from the galleries? What, then, was the visibility of similar devices in medieval practice? What problems were raised when the street performers of the Mysteries acted simultaneously between their pageant stages and the street ('Herod rages in the pageant and in the street also'; and 'the 3 kings speaketh in the street' from the Coventry plays)? Presumably, as in the former time, the spectators would be kept away from that part of the ground needed in the action. A part of the yard could be roped off. Perhaps for a play like *England's Joy*, which had an unusually high entrance fee, there were no ground spectators at all, and whole portions of the play (there was to have been 'a great triumph made with fighting of twelve gentlemen at Barriers', as well as 'the battle at Sea in '88 with England's victory') might conceivably have taken place in the yard. In any case it need not be supposed that, necessarily, for all plays, the whole of the yard was always occupied by spectators. There is more than a little reason to believe that Elizabethan stage practice did occasionally include, if only for its stunt value, a certain amount of action in the yard. The possibility alone is enough to demand research. Is it possible, for example, that the barge in the last act of *Pericles*, in which Marina and her attendants were brought out to Pericles' black-sailed ship, was a practicable boat brought in through one of the gates of the yard and moored alongside the stage, which was the ship? Also, there are a number of references, in early plays, to actors on horseback. ('Enter a spruce Courtier a horsebacke', I *Richard II*.) Sir Edmund Chambers has suggested that this effect was simulated by the use of hobby-horses on the stage, but surely it is worth investigating the alternative, that there were occasions when real horses were ridden into the yard? It could so easily have been done.

But all this takes us beyond our present scope and plunges us far too deeply into conjecture. We have here tried to show that the Shakespearean public

D

stage had its origin in the common scaffold stage of the street theatres; that, like so many of these, it was built high, sometimes head-high to the spectators standing around it, always high enough to allow working space underneath without recourse to digging a cellar; and that it was usually an open structure of posts or trestles, draped round with hangings. We suggest that these conditions were general throughout Shakespeare's time, though with ever-increasing degrees of modification (for example, it is probable that stages tended to become larger and more solidly built as the successful career of the public theatres went on), culminating in the large fully panelled-in stage of the Fortune, which, I suggest, was in some respects ahead of its time. But in any case the old style was always just around the corner, and when the Hope was built, thirteen years after the Fortune and for the same proprietors, its stage was a trestled one in the oldest manner of all.

4. The Nature of the Tiring-house

THE TIRING-HOUSE was that place at the rear of the stage in which the actors attired themselves (hence the name) and from which they came out into the action of the play. It corresponded in one sense to what we now call 'behind the scenes', but in another sense it was more than this; it was the scene itself. The word *scene* has its origin in the ancient Greek word *skēnē*, meaning a tent or booth, and was in fact, in the old Greek mime-theatre, that very same tent or booth behind the little portable stage whose persistence throughout theatrical history we have already noted.[1] In the

[1] I know of one instance in which the tiring-house of an Elizabethan theatre seems to be specifically referred to as 'the tent'. In September 1599, the German Thomas Platter visited the Curtain theatre, and saw a play in which the actors 'represented various nations, with whom on each occasion an Englishman fought for his daughter, and overcame them all except the German, who

great classical theatres of Greece and Rome the word was maintained in its original sense, though by then it referred to large permanent buildings of wood or stone. The place which the Elizabethans called the tiring-house was for the Romans, the scene; the monumental front wall of it facing the audience was the *frons scenæ*, or face of the scene; and the open area in front of this, on to which the actors came forth, was the proscenium, that is, the place in front of the scene. The Elizabethans accepted this arrangement in its classical sense. Florio, in his Dictionary (1598) has: '*Scena*. The . . . forepart of a theatre where players make them ready, being trimmed with hangings'; and in the Swan drawing (whose admitted purpose it is to point a similarity between the Elizabethan and the Classical theatre) the stage itself is correctly labelled 'Proscenium'. This original use and derivation of the scene-building or tiring-house is important to us because it is involved with the whole controversial subject of the 'inner stage', which we shall examine below. But we have first to consider how the tiring-house portion was arranged within the main building which contained it.

Most reconstructors agree that the tiring-house was a portion of the main theatre building which had been divided off from the spectators and was used entirely for 'back-stage' purposes. Since the main building was round or polygonal, it followed that if the façade or 'scenic wall' of the tiring-house were nothing but a closed-off portion following the inner line of this, without addition, it would be, in plan, a shallow curve; or, more likely in a wooden building, three flat planes in shallow oblique. This arrangement has sometimes been adopted in reconstruction. The alternative is that the scenic wall was flat, either built a little forward of the main enclosing wall, or else as a chord between the two points of its inner circumference. I myself believe that the flat scenic wall is the more likely solution, since it has the authority of the Swan drawing and of classical practice, and since it accords better with the sequence of development which I suggest in the drawings in Appendix A. There is no essential logic in a belief, which has influenced most reconstructors, that because the levels and dimensions of the main building were such and such,

---

won the daughter in fight. He then sat down with him, and gave him and his servant strong drink, so that they both got drunk, and the servant threw his shoe at his master's head and they both fell asleep. Meanwhile the Englishman went into the tent [*zelte*], robbed the German of his gains, and thus he outwitted the German also.' Of course it has to be allowed that the tent referred to might have been a special piece of setting erected on the stage. But it does not read like that to me. I offer the opinion that this passing reference to *the* tent, instead of to *a* tent, implies an accepted, more or less permanent or standard feature, which must surely be the arras- or curtain-hung tiring-house; and it implies further that this tiring-house still retained something of the character of the original booth.

therefore the levels and dimensions of the tiring-house corresponded with them. This may have been so; or it may partly have been so; but it is a characteristic of ordinary building in the Elizabethan period not so much to unify the whole as to build each unit for its own purpose, and then to close them all together in any convenient way. The dimensions of the main frame of the Fortune or the Globe do not necessarily govern the dimensions of their tiring-houses. The wording of both the Fortune and Hope contracts suggests that the tiring-houses were separately considered.

We have, then, a façade which we will assume to have been in a straight line, closing the back of the stage. We can suppose that it rose to something like the full height of the surrounding auditorium, that is of three storeys, comprising an average overall height of about 30 feet. The openings in this façade, giving onto the stage, may have differed somewhat between one play-house and another, but the conventional arrangement with which we are familiar is near enough to the style and requirements of the time to be accepted, at least as a starting point. According to this we have, on the stage level, a central opening closed in with arras or curtains, and two important doorways, one on either side of it; on the floor above this an open gallery flanked by two smaller openings or windows, sometimes represented in reconstruction as oriel or bay windows; and perhaps above this another floor with window or gallery openings.

So far, so good. Now we have to examine a popular theory that the central opening on the stage level was an 'inner stage' which was capable of being opened and closed and was constantly used in support of the forward or main stage, and that the gallery above this was called the 'upper stage', having special uses of its own. For instance, John Cranford Adams, in his book *The Globe Playhouse; its Design and Equipment*, not only prescribes for these areas an extensive and particularised range of functions around which he claims the whole method of Elizabethan play-structure was composed, but gives exact measurements into the bargain. Yet this really goes far beyond the warrant of evidence. We know, certainly, that the Elizabethans used an area which they called the 'upper stage', and this we shall discuss shortly. But we do *not* know how or to what extent they recognised such a place as an 'inner stage'. The Swan drawing does not show such a thing, and the wording 'inner stage' does not occur anywhere in the whole corpus of Elizabethan theatrical literature (as indeed it could not, for according to the Elizabethan under-standing of the word stage, such a phrase would be meaningless). The nearest equivalent known to me is the one used in a stage direction by Greene in

Alphonsus of Arragon: 'Let there be a Brazen Head set in the middle of *the place behind the stage*.' The italics are mine. I would draw attention to the fact that the occasional and auxiliary use, however often, of a place recognised as being *behind* but not *of* the stage proper, does not constitute an 'inner stage' in the sense of an alternative acting area for special purposes, such as to represent 'interior' scenes, which is the theory offered by Cranford Adams and others. The point is not a small one. It surely connotes a whole difference of character in theatrical presentation.

This is not, of course, to question that there was, connected with most if not all Elizabethan stages, a part of the rear wall which was either permanently hung with curtain or arras, or where a curtain or arras could be put up when required. The device of a 'discovery', that is the dramatic opening of curtains to show a specially arranged group or set-piece, is constant and common. The opening of the curtains to 'discover' the caskets in *The Merchant of Venice* is one example among many. Professor Thorndike, in his book *Shakespeare's Theatre*, lists 158 indisputable examples where an arrangement of curtains or arras is used in this or some similar way, and these are only a sample. Yet in none of his examples need we suppose that any important phase of action was sustained *behind* the curtain line. The curtains are used, as in the case of the caskets quoted above, to show some furnishing or tableau to the actors on the stage outside, or sometimes to house a large piece of furniture, such as a bed, to which the actors retire—as in *Romeo and Juliet*, IV, iii, where Juliet 'falls upon her bed within the curtains'. But if a bed is to feature in a more extended scene, then it is likely that instead of being left in the place behind the stage it will be thrust forward on to it. Thus we find in Middleton's *A Chaste Maid in Cheapside* the direction 'A Bed Thrust out upon the stage; Allwit's wife in it'; and in Heywood's *The Golden Age* we have 'Enter the foure old Beldams, drawing out Danae's bed: she in it', followed later in the scene by 'The bed is drawn in . . .' These are only two of many examples of the thrusting in and out of beds upon the stage. It is clear from this and other instances that there was an established practice of bringing large properties forward on to the stage in preference to having a scene take place within a curtained recess. Even though it is possible to argue that there was no hard-and-fast standardisation of method between one theatre and another or from one period to the next, it still seems to me a general rule that the action of a play, although it might look towards or enter from the tableau or set-piece revealed by the opening of the curtains, would not usually take place within the recess. If this is so, it follows that the recess need not necessarily be very wide or deep. This is exemplified by the fact that in every case where actors do in fact enter the recess for some stated requirement of the play, it is always understood as representing a small, enclosed or withdrawn place— a cell, a study, a cave or a curtained bed.

The exaggeration of the importance, and also of the size, of the so-called inner stage in many reconstructions has perhaps been due to an erroneous theory that the inner stage was the embryo of our modern proscenium stage. According to this belief, as time went on the 'inner stage' was found to have a greater and greater value in performance, so that the Elizabethan actor came to centre more and more of his action in and around it. It has been supposed that 'interior' scenes were acted in it throughout, that it began to be used not only for set-pieces but for furnished 'settings', that its size was increased until, at the Restoration, its outer frame had enveloped nearly all the original open stage and had become the 'proscenium arch' of to-day. The facts do not bear out this theory. Movable scenery, which gave rise to the proscenium arch, was not *developed* as an aid to drama upon the public stage, but was *invented*, complete, as an ingenious toy for the entertainment of the Court. When during the Restoration this invention was married to the public London theatres the actors still did not perform in the midst of it as they do to-day, but well out in front of it, upon the large apron stage which was the descendant of the open stage of Elizabethan times. The proscenium arch did then develop, but *not* by an enlargement of a former 'inner stage'. The development has been fully described by Richard Southern in his book *The Open Stage*, and I cannot do better than quote him here in full. We have already seen that the true 'proscenium' was the acting-place in front of the scene-building or tiring-house. Southern now continues:

'When, after the Elizabethan period, Davenant produced his new form of Restoration stage and theatre, he desired to add movable scenery at the back, worked by machinery. Such an introduction would normally have covered up the doors of entrance and the balconies which were formerly in the tiring-house wall—and their loss could not be tolerated since they formed an essential part of contemporary dramatic technique. Further, the new scenery demanded some sort of "frontispiece" to frame it and to mask the machinery which worked it.

'But Davenant's stage was built in a narrow hall instead of a wide polygonal ring, such as was the Elizabethan play-house, and so it presumably had to spread right across the building. That is to say the *proscaenium* (or stage) now reached to the side walls of the house. In these side walls . . . the essential doors and balconies could now be built, . . . thus giving access upon the *proscaenium* but from the sides instead of the back (which was thus left unused and free for scenery).

'What more logical than that the doors which gave upon the proscenium should be called the proscenium doors, and the walls which flanked the sides of the proscenium and held those doors should be called the proscenium sides, and that the ceiling joining the unity above should come to be called the proscenium ceiling, or top?

'Thence it is an easy step to call the whole unity . . . the "proscenium", with that shortening of phrase which is so often met in the speech of a craft or profession. Any other attempt to trace the origin of our proscenium is, I think, ill-founded.'

❖   ❖   ❖

We have already noted that the term 'inner stage' does not occur in Elizabethan texts; when, however, we come to consider the 'upper stage' we find a different case. The Elizabethans did occasionally use the term. In Day's *Humour Out of Breath* we come across the stage direction 'Re-enter Florimel and Assistance on the upper stage', followed a little later by the direction that a game of blind man's buff, from which two other characters below had been resting, 'is renewed on the lower stage'. One of many familiar examples embodying the use of the upper level occurs in *The Merchant of Venice*, II, v, where 'Enter Jessica, above, in boy's clothes'. She speaks with Lorenzo who awaits her below, throws him down a casket, then 'Exit above', then seven lines further on, 'Enter Jessica below.'

The frequent dramatic use of what seems to have been a permanent upper level is the most characteristic single feature of Elizabethan stage practice. Since it is such a peculiarity, we ought to consider not only how it was used, but also whence it was derived. These facts, if we can establish them, will help us to visualise its appearance.

The commonest and simplest form of its use is that just quoted above: one character watches, or speaks down to another character below, as from the balcony or window of a house: e.g., Juliet at her window, with Romeo below. Another common form, especially in the earlier plays of the period, is the use of the upper level as a podium from which an introductory character may comment upon the unfolding of the play below. Thus in Greene and Lodge's

Looking Glass for London & England the prophet Oseas sits throughout the play on an upper level, to which he is brought in by an angel, and from which he makes moral comments during the intervals. In Marston's *Antonio's Revenge* the ghost of Andrugio watches from above the working out of vengeance for his own death. That is simple enough. But then we turn to *The Taming of the Shrew*, and find that not only is the upper level made the place from which Christopher Sly and his 'wife' sit to watch the whole play, making comments from time to time ('would 'twere done!'), but we also find that the whole previous introductory scene of Sly's awakening in the lord's bedroom, nearly 150 lines of good comedy, takes place 'aloft'. That means that the upper level is here required to house a bed, some chairs, six actors with speaking parts, and one or two attendants. What sort of an upper level is this, in which such a scene can be effectively played to a large audience?

The upper stage is usually represented as a balustraded open gallery, continuing the line of the auditorium galleries on the middle level. Such an arrangement is well suited to the simple house-and-window scenes as those from *The Merchant of Venice* and *Romeo and Juliet* quoted above; but it surely presents difficulties when it has to cope with this scene from *The Taming of the Shrew*? I cannot feel convinced that any sustained scene can be theatrically effective if the audience has to watch it through the bars of a railing, set back as it were in the first-floor opening of a wall, especially when there is a large stage standing idle and empty below it between the spectators and the play. Yet there is a strong theory, supported by Chambers and championed in the utterance by Cranford Adams, that the upper level was always used to represent bed-chamber and upper-room scenes. Adams, for instance, would have us believe that the whole of the great scene between Hamlet and his mother, with the killing of Polonius (*Hamlet*, III, iv) was written to be played in this situation. True, in Adams' reconstruction his upper stage is very large and visible, and he takes care to space the individual rails of his railing very wide. Yet still a theory which ascribes to the Elizabethans such a hard-and-fast literal localisation (upstairs rooms must be seen to be up, and downstairs rooms seen to be down) strikes me as foreign to the general character of their drama, and I cannot personally believe that any such scene as that just quoted from *Hamlet* can have been acted anywhere but right out on the main stage. None the less, whatever may have been done in *Hamlet*, the text of *The Taming of the Shrew* clearly requires us to accept an upper stage capable of sustaining the comedy scene described. Bearing this in mind we will for the present leave it, and pass on to another instance where the use of an upper level is certain and has to be both dramatic and sustained. The instance I choose is the climax of *Antony and Cleopatra*, where the upper level is supposed to be a 'monument'. Upon this there has to be room for Cleopatra, Charmian, Iras and two or more maids. There must be space for these to haul up the dying Antony, and to lay him, presumably with good visibility for the audience, before Cleopatra; and the place should presumably be suitable for staging the whole drama and poetry of their last parting.

It is evident at once that here there can be no balustrade, since this would gravely obstruct not only the visibility of the scene of Antony's death but also the mechanical business of heaving him aloft. Since contemporary pictures of upper stages without balustrades are available (Plates 21, 27), and although it is true these do not refer specifically to the English theatre, this may be accepted at once. But there is also the question of the height of the monument above the stage. Antony has to be hauled over its edge on to the upper level by a small number of boy actors. The position for hauling is awkward. Adams suggests it was done with the aid of a pulley and ropes from above. I think rather that it was done with the sole aid of the men actors on the stage below, and that the haul was not much, if any, higher than these could reach—say between 7 and 8 feet. Was this, then, the height of the permanent upper stage?

Not necessarily: we have to consider that there may have been some impermanent special structure erected to serve as a monument. Let me conjecture how this might be done.

The conditions I wish to fulfil are, first, to have this scene not too far back from the audience: thus I would like to bring the monument structure somewhat forward from the tiring-house wall. Second, Cleopatra and her maids must be able to enter and leave the monument while still remaining on an upper level. Third, they must have a fair amount of room. Fourth, they must not be much beyond the reach of the men on the lower stage. And fifth, their position must make some sense out of the following curious passage in the text: In Act IV, xv, Cleopatra, having just entered on to the monument, is approached by Diomedes, below. She speaks down to him, concerning Antony:

> How now! Is he dead?
>
> *Diomedes*: His death's upon him, but not dead.
> Look out o' the other side your monument;
> His guard have brought him thither.
>
> *Enter, below, Antony, borne by the Guard.*

Thus we find that Cleopatra is to look out first on one side of the monument, and then on the other.

The sketch below fulfils all these requirements in a manner which I think simple and consistent with Elizabethan ideas. A small temporary upper

stage has been built against the tiring-house façade, in front of the stage gallery, which here has no balustrade. It juts out on to the stage between the two main tiring-house doors, so that Diomedes, entering at one door, indicates that Antony is being carried in at the other, 'o' the other side your monument'. At the end of the scene the women bear Antony's body away through the gallery at the back. There follows one scene in Caesar's camp, and thereafter the play returns to end in the monument. I must say that I do not think that this final scene was actually played *upon* the monument in the same way as before, but rather that most of it, if not all, took place on the main stage, the monument being understood. If it were done 'aloft', however (which the text does not indicate), the arrangement described would still serve best.

This small temporary structure which we have just used for a monument is worth consideration in other ways. If hung with curtains it could serve well for many of the purposes which have usually been ascribed to the 'inner stage'. It would thus bring those necessary effects which are usually thrust back into 'the place behind the stage', forward and on to it, into the midst of the action. For instance, in *Pericles*, V, i, the scene opens on board Pericles' ship, off Mytilene. We have already been told by Gower, the Chorus of the play, that the stage itself represents the ship. A stage direction then tells us that there is: 'A pavilion on deck, with a curtain before it; Pericles within it, reclined on a couch.' Our structure could be this pavilion. Or, on other occasions, wreathed with greenery it could become that favourite Elizabethan stage property, an arbour, such as that arbour in which Benedick hides himself and overhears the talk of Beatrice's love for him (*Much Ado About Nothing*, II, iii). Such a structure, if it were commonly used, might help to explain why no permanently curtained 'inner stage' is shown in the Swan drawing.

My argument for suggesting that such a fit-up structure was used has been so far only that it would have helped to bring the business of the rear alcove and of the upper stage forward into the principal acting area. On this alone I might have thought twice about suggesting it, were it not for two things. First, I find that Professor G. F. Reynolds, after a close analysis in his book, *The Staging of Elizabethan Plays at the Red Bull Theatre*, has come to a similar conclusion, and gives many examples of the textual and theatrical aptness of such a fit-up. Sir Edmund Chambers, too, is prepared to accept it, speaking of the possibility of 'some porch-like projection from the back wall' which may have been supported by posts; and Cranford Adams has conjectured such a feature as being an intermediate development in the structure of playhouses. But secondly, if the proposition made in the foregoing chapter may be accepted, i.e., that the Elizabethan public stage was developed from the booth or street theatres, then in the course of that development there could well have been a time when the curtained booth, once the tiring-house itself, would have stood on the enlarged new stage of the permanent theatre, and up against the wall of the permanent tiring-house, with just the appearance of the little pavilion I have described. Being no longer necessary as a tiring-house, it might now have been dismantled, but since it was a part of the actor's traditional equipment, and likely to be used again whenever the company went out into the provinces, it would be kept handy in the store-room.

The growth of the stage and tiring-house of an Elizabethan public theatre along these lines is sketched in Appendix A. I do not, of course, pretend that these drawings are anything more than conjectural, but I believe that the truth lies somewhere within the field which they cover.

❖ ❖ ❖

It will now be of interest to consider a certain problem of the upper stage which usually causes controversy among students of the subject—largely, perhaps, because it will not fit conveniently into any hard-and-fast scheme of reconstruction. There is in Middleton's *Family of Love* a remark by one of the characters who says that he went to a play at the Fortune, where he 'saw Sampson bear the town-gates on his neck from the lower to the upper stage'. W. J. Lawrence quotes this among other examples which gives him to think that there must have been some sort of staircase connecting the lower to the upper stage, in full view of the audience. Among other instances he gives the scene in *Julius Caesar*, V, iii, where Pindarus mounts a 'hill' to spy out the battle for Cassius, and then descends at his request to kill him. Cranford Adams refutes this latter example, but the former stands. I would add to it another, which occurs in the *Plot of the Play called England's Joy*, already referred to in Chapter 3. Here, in the second incident of the action, Queen Elizabeth enters and takes her throne, which is 'attended with Peace, Plenty, and Civil Policy; a sacred prelate standing at her right hand, betokening the serenity of the Gospel; at her left hand Justice; and at her feet War, with a scarlet robe of peace upon his armour; a wreath of bays about his temples, and a branch of palm in his hand'. Here, in fact, is a tableau which students of the Renaissance theatre will recognise at once as a 'Throne of Honour'. It accords (as indeed does the whole description of the play) with the full formal and allegorical method of presentation made familiar by contemporary paintings and engravings, and which has been studied at length by G. R. Kernodle in his important book *From Art to Theatre*. An actual example from the London of 1604—only two years after the business of *England's Joy*— can be seen in Plate 31, where the central tableau under the title Londinium represents the Throne of Monarchia Britannica, supported on either side by the virtues of Gladness, Veneration, Vigilance, Unanimity and the rest. At her feet, where War had been in *England's Joy*, sits in this instance Divine Wisdom. There is nothing at first to suggest in the *England's Joy* text that the throne was supposed to be raised up like this, though from study of other instances one might already take it for granted. But then in the fourth episode there enters a cruel Tyrant (Spain) who mangles and wounds a beautiful Lady (Belgia) 'and so leave her bloody, with her hair about her shoulders, lying upon the ground. To her come certain gentlemen, who seeing her piteous despoilment, turn to the Throne of England, *from whence one descendeth*, taketh up the Lady, wipeth her eyes, bindeth up her wounds . . .', etc. It does not, of course, follow that this throne would have been presented on the upper stage. I only offer the suggestion, since it suggests itself so strongly to me, that such a throne could have been set upon the top of a rostrum like that discussed above for Cleopatra's monument, with an ascent arranged on either side as in the triumphal archway in Plate 31. It would thus be not only in the full Elizabethan style, but far less ambitious than the 'high throne, wherein the King should sit, . . . proudly placed with two and twenty degrees to the top'[1] which Chambers accepts as typical, in spirit at least, of the Elizabethan stage. In Dekker's *Old Fortunatus* there is a dream scene where Fortune ascends to her throne: 'Fortune takes her Chair, the Kings lying at her feet, she treading on them as she goes up.' And presently: 'She comes down.' In *Richard III*, IV, ii, King Richard enters in pomp, and bids Buckingham:

> Give me thy hand. [*Here he ascendeth the throne*]
> Thus high, by thy advice
> And thy assistance is King Richard seated . . .

How high was this? Was it high in metaphor only? It suggests to me that an upper stage may have been used for this and perhaps other formal throne scenes, with steps approaching it from the lower one.

But what, then, was the usual height of the upper stage? I have already questioned whether the lower-stage alcove need have been so wide as it is often represented. It is also possible that the upper stage was not raised so high. Twelve feet is frequently suggested, since that is the height of the corresponding gallery section of the auditorium, according to the Fortune and Hope contracts. Yet if it is also true that the upper stage was used to represent city or castle walls, as all commentators think they were, what are we to suppose in those cases where actors leap over or off these 'walls'? Twelve feet is a considerable drop. I cannot feel it likely that the boy who played

[1] From *The English Wagner Book*, 1594.

Arthur in *King John*, IV, iii, when he had to leap down, was expected to leap from such a height, even with a heap of rushes or some other such thing to break his fall. It is true he has to be supposed as jumping from a precipitous height, and that he kills himself by it, but since all this was conveyed to the audience by conventional and not literal means, the convention would hold equally well for a lower jump, say between 7 and 8 feet.

The extent to which purely conventional practices were used on the Elizabethan stage is not possible to determine, but we know for certain that they were used very widely, and we are more likely to be right, when faced with a puzzling stage situation, if we assume that it was disposed of by some convention of even nursery-like determine, rather than by some elaboration of theatre building which would have given a greater physical realism to the scene. We know that some Elizabethan plays were conducted according to the medieval system of 'houses', thrones and other set pieces standing simultaneously on the stage throughout the whole performance, as shown in Plate 15. This is more characteristic of the earlier groups of plays than of the Jacobean ones, though Reynolds demonstrates a probability that such methods were still used at the Red Bull as late as the second decade of the seventeenth century. We have therefore to allow for a possibility that these city and castle 'walls' may sometimes have been pieces of practicable scenery placed on the stage; yet it still remains possible that in most instances the ordinary upper stage was used, and that in the case of the *King John* scene of Arthur's leap it was not likely to have been very high.

For dramatic purposes a conventional simplification may sometimes be used even at the expense of the literal meaning of the text. In Jonson's *The Devil Is An Ass* there is a scene (II, ii) between Wittipol and Mistress Fitzdottrel which is supposed to take place as if at the upper windows of two neighbouring houses. If one were to interpret the original staging of this scene from the context of the spoken words only (to say nothing of the stage direction: 'Mrs. Fitzdottrel appears at a window of her house fronting that of Manly's Chambers') one would have no choice but to suppose that these windows faced one another, as if across a street, and it seems evident that that is what was in Jonson's mind when he was writing the play. In the 1632 edition of the text, however, Jonson tells us in the margin how the scene was actually done at the Blackfriars. It was 'acted at two windo's, as out of two contiguous buildings', and so very contiguous are they that we find as the scene proceeds that Wittipol 'grows more familiar in his Courtship, playes with her paps, kisseth her hands, etc.' Clearly it was theatrically more effective to play the scene like this, rather than to have the characters framed in their windows at some distance from one another for the whole length of the scene.

The clear information we derive from this scene, therefore, is as follows. The scene was played by adopting a convention which was presumably acceptable to both audience and author, even though it did to some extent contradict the text. The scene was 150 lines long, as long, that is, as the upper-stage scene from *The Taming of the Shrew* which we have been considering above. Four characters appear at the windows at one time and another, two in each.

One wonders, then, how these windows were arranged at the Blackfriars. Presumably, in order to be seen from, and to have command of, all parts of the house, they would have been centred in the rear wall of the stage, like the windows in the Roxana engraving (Plate 45). In this case the actors would have been visible only from the waist upwards. We can accept this if we must, although it would have been hampering for the actors. There is, however, an alternative solution which suggests itself to me from a remark made by Mistress Fitzdottrel referring to these windows during a previous scene. She speaks of 'The Gentleman's chamber-window in Lincoln's Inn there, that opens to my gallery'. What *gallery* is she referring to? Is it not possible that there was a small balcony with a railing round it in front of each window; or, come to that, one balcony running across the front of the two windows merely divided off in the middle; so that the characters coming out from each window could conveniently look into each other's houses, or embrace each other as required by the text? If so we are back again at our little porch or booth. The engraving reproduced in Plate 49 of the Schouwburg in Amsterdam, although of a later date (1658), shows a small central, porch-like upper stage of this kind in an indoor theatre.

Whichever way this window scene was done, however, it is clear that it was done in a fairly confined space. So perhaps after all the same condition could have applied to the bed-chamber scene of the awakening of Sly in *The Taming of the Shrew*; perhaps after all we do not need all that space and furnishing we had at first supposed. *The Shrew* was also acted here, at this same Blackfriars, under the same windows, with perhaps that same gallery which exposed Mistress Fitzdottrel's adventure. And if it did not need much space at the Blackfriars, it can hardly have needed much more over the river at the Globe. The play itself derives from the style of the Italian Comedians, whose typical acting background was, once again, the familiar booth stage of the fairs. So once again I will allow myself to imagine the porch-like booth hung with its arras, standing between the two tiring-house doors. It backs up to the gallery floor, where, behind closed curtains, Sly lies snoring. A light stairway leads up on one side, and up this from below come the servants with apparel, basin and ewer. They are now standing on top of the porch-booth in front of the curtain which represents the bed. They draw the curtain. Sly emerges. 'For God's sake', he groans, 'a pot of small ale.' And so it begins. I cannot make up my mind, though, whether there would have been a railing or not.

❖ ❖ ❖

While I am engaged in this conjecture I will add a footnote to it. Ben Jonson as a playwright is notable among his contemporaries as an innovator of stage technique. His deliberate method was to use his stage as a physical unity and to base his plays upon an acceptance of the fabric as it stood, as he did in *The Alchemist*, which is a unique example for its time of a play written entirely in and around one supposed house. Now, bearing this in mind, it is interesting to consider the following facts about *Bartholemew Fair*. The play was produced at the Hope. We know that the Hope had a movable stage on trestles, in the manner of the street theatres. Theatres of this type were also commonly seen at fairs; they were, as we have seen, little trestled stages with booths at the back of them. In *Bartholemew Fair*, then, the whole of the play, after the first scene, takes place *at* the Fair, and upon a trestled stage, which, as the text of the play makes absolutely clear, was for this presentation backed by something resembling a row of booths. I suggest that Ben Jonson was suiting his play to his theatre, and that it was his intention to use the fair-booth structure of the stage, as it stood, to assist the atmosphere of his play.

Arbour
Tomb
Throne
City Walls
and Gates
Green bank

5. The Stately-Furnished Scene

THE criticism by Richard Flecknoe, in Restoration days, about the
'plain and simple' methods of Shakespeare's theatre, as having no
scenery 'nor Decorations of the Stage, but onely old Tapestry and
the Stage strewed with Rushes', has been more often quoted and had
a much wider effect than the somewhat contradictory statement with which he
followed it: 'For Scenes and Machines they are no new invention, our Masks
and some of our Plays in former times (though not so ordinary) having had
as good or rather better than we have now.' In Victorian times the 'plain and
simple' view went unchallenged, though with it there went a puritanical
approval of plainness and simplicity. The anonymous author of a popular
educational work, *Old England*, published about 1857, may be taken as typical.
He writes of the fire which ended the career of the first Globe, a fire which,
as is known, was started by some burning material from a theatre cannon
which was shot accidentally into the thatched roof. 'The clumsy management of the cannons', says the writer, 'and the *thatched* theatre, shows how
comparatively unfamiliar were those who first witnessed the representation

of the most wonderful series of plays the world has seen, with those costly and laboured contrivances to which in our day the soul of the art has been sacrificed. Poetry, wit, passion, humour, wisdom, could be relished by our ancestors without them. . . . One illustration of the stage ceremony of our ancestors is delightful for its almost infantine simplicity. In Greene's *Pinner of Wakefield* two parties are quarrelling: "Come, Sir," says one; "will you come to the town's end, now?" "Ay, Sir, come," replies his adversary. And in the next line, having, we may suppose, made as distant a movement as the narrow stage admitted of, he continues, with amusing faith in the imaginative power of the audience, "Now, we are at the town's end, what shall we say now?"'

We nowadays do not necessarily regard such methods as 'infantine', and indeed the imaginative powers of modern audiences have been well schooled in every kind of theatrical style and convention. Yet the writer just quoted was evidently a discerning man, and it is at first hard for us to suppose that he was far wrong about the simplicity of the Globe when one remembers the matter of that thatched roof. The thatch, the tapestry and the rush-strewn stage: there come into the mind's eye the unmistakable features of a cottage—can it be Anne Hathaway's? And below the thatch one imagines the quaint criss-cross of Old English half-timbering—can it be Shakespeare's birthplace in Henley Street, Stratford? One recalls the inn-yards where the players used to act; the rumbustious scene paints itself for us in the manner of a Christmas card, and persuades us to accept its implied simplicity of manner because it is so picturesque in effect. But is this, after all, the right effect? Until quite recently it used to be believed that Shakespeare's plays were originally acted in the ordinary costume of his own day. This we now know to be untrue—or at least a very misleading over-simplification—but it is still widely taught that the architectural background of the stage in Shakespeare's theatre was deliberately intended to give the impression of the normal domestic architecture of the day. Adams, in *The Globe Playhouse*, takes this for granted. 'The façade of the tiring-house', he says, 'differed from its model, *a short row of London houses*, mainly in having . . . curtains suspended in the middle'.[1] But there is no reason at all for supposing that any feature of an Elizabethan playhouse was ever based on any such model. The idea is contrary to the very nature of Elizabethan drama. It is true that there was an important group of Elizabethan plays which dealt with the contemporary scene; but the great majority of their drama was otherwise. Of Shakespeare's thirty-seven plays not one was set in the England of his own day: all were

[1] Adams, *The Globe Playhouse*, p. 135. The italics are mine.

evocations of the romantic past or the romantic distance, or both; and all were intentionally so. Not even *Twelfth Night*, which one would take to be very contemporary and English in feeling, was allowed to come nearer home than Illyria. One may say that this was merely a nod in the direction of the prevailing Italianate fashion; but, even so, that fashion was itself the fashion of the splendid and romantic scene, and was the vein which inspired the greater part of all the work of every dramatist of the time except Ben Jonson; and even he, the great exemplar of English social satire, produced many works in a heroic or romantic mode. Temples, palaces and towers were the characteristic backgrounds of the Elizabethan drama; the theatre was a place for 'Heroick and Majestique recreacions'.[1] Therefore, unless it can be shown that Elizabethan managers and actors were ignorant of any architecture but that of their own streets, or else had not the means or the imagination to provide themselves with any other, we ought surely to suppose that their theatres were furnished in a style at least suggestive of some sort of fantasy and splendour. In fact, we know that the imagination, the means and the style were all at hand. And since a robust and fanciful ostentation has been typical of all popular entertainment from the most ancient times, one would surely expect to find evidence of it on the Elizabethan stage, of all stages.

The evidence is not lacking. 'Behold,' cries the preacher Thomas White, 'behold the sumptuous theatre houses, a continual monument of London's prodigality and folly.' He goes on to say that they are schools of vice, dens of thieves and theatres of all lewdness, and if his testimony stood alone one might well brush aside his mention of sumptuousness as the exaggeration of a zealous Puritan who could not tell the difference between a piece of tinsel and an orgiastic carouse. But it does not stand alone. Here is another Puritan, John Stockwood, declaiming in 1578 against 'the gorgeous playing place erected in the fields'. Sumptuous and gorgeous already; and then a year or two later Stephen Gosson, in a pamphlet written against the theatres, still has to allow 'the beauty of the houses and the stages'; while Thomas Nashe in another, defending them, says, 'Our Scene is more stately furnished than ever it was in the time of Roscius . . .'

The quotations given above range over a period from 1577, the year after the first theatre was built, until 1592. Since the theatres continued to prosper and were increasingly patronised by people of taste and culture, it is hardly likely that they decreased in splendour as time went on; and when in 1611

---

[1] This phrase is found in the prospectus of an Amphitheatre which was under consideration in 1620. Cf. Leslie Hotson, *The Projected Amphitheatre*, in *Shakespeare Survey 2*.

Thomas Coryat published, in his *Crudities*, an account of his travels in Europe, he had this to say of a theatre he visited in Venice: 'I was at one of their play-houses, where I saw a comedy acted. The house is very beggarly and base in comparison of our stately play-houses in England: neither can their actors compare with us for apparel, shews and music.'

Defenders and detractors alike, then, agree in this, that the theatres were decked out in some sort of splendour, and Nashe even believed the London theatres to have outrivalled the admired model of Imperial Rome. For in fact the Roman model, so far as there was a model at all, was the one. Johannes de Witt, the Flemish visitor to the Swan whose report originated the famous drawing, was particularly struck, as we have seen, by what he considered a resemblance between that theatre and a Roman original, and the drawing is annotated with the corresponding classical references, expressly to point the fact. Ben Jonson, whose classically minded approach to the theatre was famous, has given us on the title-page of the 1616 edition of his Works, a picture of a classical 'theatrum' as he supposed it to have appeared (Plate 43). The picture is clearly founded upon information from antiquarian sources, but the English engraver has restored it to what he and/or Ben Jonson must have supposed was its proper original form, by the addition of some huts over the top, after the style of those familiar huts over the theatres on Bankside.

Edmund Spenser, in his *Thalia*, speaks of 'the painted theatres'. Johannes de Witt speaks also of painting: he says that the Swan was 'supported by wooden columns, painted in such excellent imitation of marble that it might deceive even the most prying observer'. This is momentous information, but before following it up, let us look at another aspect of theatre painting. We have already noted in Chapter II that that roof called the Heavens, over the stage, is believed to have been ornamentally painted, probably with stars, suns, moons, or with allegorical and zodiacal figures. Adams quotes a fascinating list of references to the painted ceiling above the actors' heads, as for instance this from Dekker's *The Whore of Babylon*:

> 3 *King*: Can yonder roof, that's nailed so fast with stars
>   Cover a head so impious, and not crack?

and from Massinger's *Very Woman*:

> *Almira*: —But look yonder!
>   Amongst a million of glorious lights
>   That deck the heavenly canopy, I have
>   Discerned his soul, transformed into a star.
>   Do you not see it?

Leonora: Lady!
Almira: Look with my eyes.
What splendour circles it! The heavenly archer
Not far off distant, appears dim with envy,
Viewing himself outshined.

A similar reference occurs in *The Silent Woman*, III, i. Captain Otter, the hen-pecked sportsman, is complaining of his wife's unreasonable attitude in the matter of bulls and bears. His friend Clerimont says:

Cler.: Ay, she must hear argument. Did not Pasiphae, who was a queen, love a bull: And was not Calisto . . . turn'd into a bear, and made a star, mistress Ursula, in the heavens?
Otter: O lord! that I could have said as much!
I will have these stories painted in the Bear-garden, *ex Ovidii metamorphosi*.

If this is not a reference to a painted Heavens in the Bear-garden it must refer to some other painted decorations there (presumably of classical subjects) which were topical at the time of the play's original production, either because they were just being done or else because they were in some special way a feature of that house; one might suppose them as being painted around the parapet of the middle gallery, very like those scenes that are painted in a primitive and boisterous style upon the fascias of roundabouts and booths at fairgrounds to-day. Indeed, one should bear this style always in mind when imagining the ornament of the Elizabethan stage. One should be on one's guard against supposing a refinement of taste beyond what a journeyman painter could do out of his copy-book. A good example of the vernacular style of painting in the period can be seen in Plate 56, and it falls very aptly upon the present subject, for it shows nothing less than a ceiling painted as a Heavens, still existing to-day in its original colours. Here we see, among cushiony white clouds, allegorical figures of the sort referred to in the plays, and behind them a blue firmament 'nail'd so fast with stars'. It is very likely indeed that just such a painting as this stood out over the stage at the Globe, and if so, this ceiling may be regarded as a unique original relic, at one remove, of the Elizabethan stage.

This ceiling is believed to be the work of itinerant Flemish painters,[1] which in itself would be typical of the time in England. Almost the whole taste of painting, engraving and architecture in Elizabethan and Jacobean England was influenced by the Flemish style, even when it was not actually executed

[1] Cf. article by Oliver Hill in *Country Life* for Jan. 23, 1948.

by Flemish artists. The names of Visscher, Hondius and Gheeraerts meet us at every turn of portraiture or topography. Shakespeare's own portrait is by Martin Droeshout, a Fleming settled in London; and it is Johannes de Witt,

A dais with 'balusters' painted on flat boards. This not only indicates the style of popular ornamentation likely at the theatres, but also suggests the treatment of the gallery palings at the Swan (cf. Plate 7)
(From Turberville's *Noble Arte of Venerie*, 1576)

the Flemish traveller, who tells us of the marble-painted pillars at the Swan. So we take up this detail again, which I referred to above as momentous information, and following it we find that it leads us again to Flanders, for the use of wooden columns painted like marble was very common in the decoration of Flemish theatres. A feature of Flemish town life at this time was its traditional theatre, which was organised by private societies called 'Chambers of Rhetoric' or 'Rederyker' Societies. It was their business to celebrate great public occasions by performances or recitals in verse and music, upon stages specially designed in a (usually) sumptuous baroque style. The appearance of these stages has been recorded in many engravings, and it was as long ago as 1889 that Wilhelm Creizenach suggested that there was an important connexion between these stages and the theatre of Shakespeare's London. It is surprising that so little notice was taken of his opinion at the time, but of recent years the trend of research has come with more and more emphasis to confirm his view. Here, surely, is the 'Heroick and Majestique' style we have been seeking, and it is not only confined to the engravings of theatres and triumphal arches in the streets of Brussels and Antwerp, for some of the most elaborate examples of it were erected not in Flanders at all, but as triumphal arches in the streets of London to celebrate the coronation procession of James I in 1604. These grandiose façades were embellished with allegorical devices by Dekker, Middleton and Jonson; Edward Alleyn appeared as the Genius of the City to speak the verses of welcome to the King; and Shakespeare himself, with the other members of his Company, the King's Men, received a bounty of scarlet cloth to make his livery for the occasion.

Some of these triumphal arches are shown in Plates 29 to 34, and they should be compared not only with the examples from Flanders (Plates 27, 28) but also with the ornamental title pages to English books (Plates 42, 43). This was the accepted high style of the time, and it would indeed be surprising if it had not found its way into the playhouses.

The theatres were prosperous, scenic painters and builders were available with their Flemish copy-books at hand; the baroque style was paramount, the audience expected it, and actors everywhere else in Europe flourished in it. Moreover, our particular evidence confirms the detail of marbled and allegorical painting, and of sumptuousness in the Elizabethan theatre. In view of all this it should be difficult to prove, not that this was in fact the style with which the Elizabethan stage was embellished, but rather that any other style was ever likely to have been considered.

Upon stages of this sort, then, arrayed with pillars, pilasters, posts and 'carved proportions', painted in marbling and in bright colours, picked out with gilding and hung with arras and curtains, the plays were mounted. We are well informed of the accessories that further enriched them. We know the details of Henslowe's property room at the Rose, from his famous inven-

tory of March 1598. I here reprint the selection given in modern spelling by
Dr. G. B. Harrison:[1]

i rock, i cage, i tomb, i Hell mouth.
i tomb of Guido, i tomb of Dido, i bedstead.
viii lances, i pair of stairs for Phaeton.
ii steeples, & i chime of bells, & i beacon.
i heifer for the play of Phaeton, the limbs dead.
i globe, & i golden sceptre; iii clubs.
ii marchpanes, & the City of Rome.
i golden fleece; ii rackets; i bay tree.
i wooden hatchet; i leather hatchet.
i wooden canopy; old Mahomet's head.
i lion skin; i bear's skin; & Phaeton's limbs & Phaeton's chariot; & Argus' head.
Neptune's fork and garland.
i 'crosers' staff; Kent's wooden leg.
Iris head, & rainbow; i little altar.
viii visards; Tamberlain's bridle; i wooden mattock.
Cupid's bow, & quiver; the cloth of the Sun & Moon.
i boar's head & Cerberus' iii heads.
i Caduceus; ii moss banks, & i snake.
ii fanes of feathers; Bellendon stable; i tree of golden apples; Tantalus' tree; ix iron
     targets.
i copper target, & xvii foils.
iiii wooden targets; i greeve armour.
i sign for Mother Redcap; i buckler.
Mercury's wings; Tasso's picture; i helmet with a dragon; i shield, with iii lions;
     i elm bowl.
i chain of dragons; I gilt spear.
ii coffins; i bull's head; and i 'vylter'.
iii timbrels; I dragon in Faustus.
i lion; ii lion heads; i great horse with his legs; i sackbut.
i wheel and frame in the Siege of London.
i pair of wrought gloves.
i Pope's mitre.
iii Imperial crowns; i plain crown.
i ghost's crown; i crown with a sun.
i frame for the heading in Black Joan.
i black dog.
i cauldron for the Jew.

One hesitates to rifle this rich store for items to comment upon, but certain
of them may require it. It should be noted that the 'Hell mouth' and the

[1] *Introducing Shakespeare*, by G. B. Harrison, p. 85.

To cut off ones head, and to laie it in a platter,
which the iugglers call the decollation of Iohn Baptiſt.

The forme
of ẙ planks,
&c.

The order
of the acti-
on, as it is
to be ſhew-
ed.

'A frame for the heading'
(From Reginald Scot's *The Discoverie of Witchcraft*, 1584)

'dragon in Faustus', for example, come straight from the medieval stage; that the 'City of Rome' and the 'cloth of the Sun & Moon', give rise to the idea of a limited use of painted pictorial backgrounds in certain circumstances (Heywood, in the *Iron Age*, made use of a Trojan horse which may also have been painted upon a cloth of this kind). The 'cauldron for the Jew', which must have been the cauldron into which Barabas falls at the end of *The*

Jew of Malta; and the 'frame for the heading' was, as Dr. Harrison explains, a piece of stage machinery to produce the illusion of a beheading. It is interesting to compare this with the woodcut reproduced opposite, which shows an old stage trick for appearing to knock off a man's head and serve it up on a platter.

In this connexion the Elizabethan taste for gory realism should be mentioned. In their frequent scenes of battle, murder and sudden death, the actors used to carry hidden bladders of pig's blood which spouted forth when they were pricked. They staged scenes of execution in which the entrails of animals bought from the slaughter-houses were plucked out from the 'victims' and exhibited to the spectators, as was done in earnest at the hanging, drawing and quartering of victims by the executioner at Tyburn. Audiences were well able to reconcile all this with their 'heroic and majestic recreations', and liked to see 'a Hector all besmeared in blood, trampling upon the bulkes of Kinges; a Troilus returning from the field, in the sight of his father Priam, as if man and horse, even from the steed's rough fetlockes to the plume on the champion's helmet, had bene together plunged into a purple ocean; to see a Pompey ride in triumph, than a Caesar conquer that Pompey; labouring Hannibal alive, hewing his passage through the Alpes. To see as I have seene, Hercules, in his owne shape, hunting the boare, knocking down the bull, taming the hart, fighting with Hydra, murdering Geryon, slaughtering Diomed, wounding the Stymphalides, killing the Centaurs, pashing the lion, squeezing the dragon, dragging Cerberus in chaynes, and lastly, on his high pyramides waiting *Nil ultra*, Oh, these were sights to make an Alexander!' So wrote Thomas Heywood in *An Apology for Actors*, and he was writing not only of what he had seen (as he said) but of what he himself created upon the stage. In his tetralogy of *The Four Ages* there was enacted a long series of the deeds of Jupiter, Hercules, Jason, Meleager and other heroes from the beginnings of Olympus to the burning of Troy and 'the deaths of Agamemnon, Menelaus, Clitemnestra, Helena, Orestes, Egistus, Pillades, King Diomed, Pyrhus, Cethus, Synon, Thersites &c.' This cycle of more than Wagnerian proportions was very popular at the time when Shakespeare was writing *Cymbeline* and *The Tempest*, and continued to be put on at one theatre or another for many years. These four plays had little literary merit, and one may suppose their popularity lay principally in their abundance of spectacle. Their stage directions show, if nothing else, the stuff the Jacobean theatre was made of. Here, for example, are some taken at random:

Enter Busyris with his Guard and Priests to sacrifice; to them two strangers, Busyris takes them and kils them upon the Altar; enter Hercules disguis'd, Busyris sends his

Guard to apprehend him, Hercules discouering himselfe beates the Guard, kils Busyris, and sacrificeth him upon the Altar, at which there fals a shower of raine, the Priests offer Hercules the Crowne of Aegypt which he refuseth. (*The Brazen Age.*)

Two fiery Buls are discovered, the Fleece hanging over them, and the Dragon sleeping beneath them: Medea with strange fiery-workes, hangs above in the Aire in the strange habite of a Conjuresse. (*The Brazen Age.*)

Sounde a dumbe shew. Enter the three fatall sisters, with a rocke, a threed, and a paire of sheeres; bringing in a Gloabe, in which they put three lots. Jupiter drawes heaven; at which Iris descends and presents him with his Eagle, Crowne and Scepter, and his thunder-bolt. Jupiter first ascends upon the Eagle, and after him Ganimed. (*The Golden Age.*)

Sound. Pluto drawes hell: the Fates put upon him a burning Roabe, and present him with a Mace, and burning crowne. (*The Golden Age.*)

Hercules sinkes himselfe. Flashes of fire; the Divels appeare at every corner of the stage with several fire-workes. The Judges of hell, and the three sisters run over the stage, Hercules after them: fire-workes all over the house. Enter Hercules. (*The Silver Age.*)

Hercules kils the Sea-Monster, the Trojans on the walles, the Greekes below. (*The Silver Age.*)

These four plays were unusual in the great amount of spectacle which they offered, but there seems to have been nothing unusual in the means used to present it. The chief mechanical aids were the flying throne which brought down the gods from the Heavens, or else the stage trap which let the devils out from Hell. For the latter it is interesting to note how, for all the classical predilections of the age, and the then available knowledge, which was not negligible, of the modes and manners of antiquity, the presumably classical Hades into which Hercules descended in *The Brazen Age* was inhabited by the same snout-faced, horn-and-claw devils, all fizzing with squibs, which Marlowe had used in *Doctor Faustus* and which were the popular stock-in-trade the theatres had inherited from the Middle Ages. Shakespeare called only twice upon this inheritance, in his first play and in his last. In 1 *Henry VI* there are the Fiends which enter with thunder at the summons of La Pucelle; and in *The Tempest* there is Caliban, the 'freckled whelp hag-born—not honoured with a human shape', whose costume we know had fishy scales upon it. He was after all only a development of the old Vice, the comic devil of the Morality Plays, in a Renaissance setting.

Shakespeare was not an innovator, as Ben Jonson was, and he was generally content to use material as he found it within the prevailing fashions of the theatre. But he did not have much use—and may, like Jonson, have had only scorn—for the Heaven and Hell devices of the popular stage. Both he and Jonson did, however, sometimes make use of the Hell trap in the conventional way for bringing in ghosts and apparitions, and there are two instances in Shakespeare of the use of the flying machine—though both of these are almost certainly interpolations by another hand, catering to the popular taste. The first is in *Macbeth*, III, v, where Hecate flies aloft seated in a 'foggy cloud'; and the second is in *Cymbeline*, V, iv, where Jupiter descends mounted on an eagle. It is interesting to note that Heywood's use of this effect in *The Brazen Age*, as given in the stage direction above, dates from within one year of the first production of *Cymbeline*, so that, if one production did not influence the other, both must have been availing themselves of a then fashionable invention.[1] Another point in this scene from *Cymbeline* is that in this case the Heavens ceiling through which the machine came down appears not to have been painted like the sky after the usual fashion, but with marbling; for, as Jupiter ascends and disappears through it, one of the characters on the stage below says: 'The marble pavement closes, he is entered his radiant roof.'[2]

One has only to visualise for a moment what the spectacular dumb shows in Heywood's *Ages* plays must have looked like in reality, bearing in mind what a lot of them there were to be got through in each play, to realise that they must have been dealt with in a very summary fashion. It was all very much of a pasteboard parade; but it is from studying the constant factors of popular taste at this level, rather than the masterpieces of exceptional men like Shakespeare and Jonson, that we are likely to learn most about the basic character of this theatre. We find that it was violent, ornate, fantastic, abundant in poetic and processional emblems, and very noisy. Some of the effects which the Elizabethans set out to achieve were so far removed from our own tastes that they cannot be judged by our theatrical standards at all. For instance, we should miss altogether the significance of the emblematic imagery which it was an intellectual fad of that time to read and decipher. 'Enter Rumour, painted full of tongues', is an image which we understand at once when seen *in words* at the beginning of 2 *Henry IV*, but it may be

---

[1] There is a design by Inigo Jones showing Jupiter mounted on an eagle in the masque *Tempe Restored*, in 1632.

[2] This tallies in an interesting way with a further reference, in *Timon of Athens*, IV, iii, where Timon speaks of Heaven as 'the marbled mansion all above'. I suppose one must be on one's guard against reading too much into such metaphors, but I am inclined to wonder whether, since both *Cymbeline* and *Timon* are dated at about the time when the King's Men began to play at the 'private' Blackfriars theatre, a Heavens there might have been a marbled one.

doubted whether we should at once 'read' the significance of the costume if it were newly shown to us, without a written explanation, on the stage. Fame with her trumpet, or sometimes for good measure with two (see Plates 25 and 45), we can easily understand, but Shame with a *black* trumpet, in the early play of *Cambyses*, has a distinction we might miss.

This emblematic method was particularly applicable to the design of costumes, and was developed to a high degree in masques and other courtly shows, so that the details of which a dress was composed might be studied, and its symbols well digested by the spectator. Thus the figure representing Sleep in *The Vision of Twelve Goddesses*, a Court masque given in 1604, was shown wearing 'a white thin Vesture cast over a black, to signify both the day and the night, with wings of the same colour, a Garland of Poppy on his head; and instead of his ivory and transparent horn, he was shewed bearing a black wand in his left hand and a white in the other'. What nowadays should we make of those white and black wands, with their distant classical reference to the Gates of Horn and Ivory which opened from the House of Dreams?

It is appropriate to bring in some mention of the Court Masques at this point, because although they were in themselves an exceptional and luxurious form of private entertainment, not of the same family or derivation as the public stage, yet their forms and methods were reflected on the public stage, and their poetic references were common to both. The masque which Shakespeare introduced into *The Tempest* was conceived in the same terms as the masques at Whitehall, and indeed the only recorded performance of the play during Shakespeare's lifetime took place at Whitehall before the King. We may therefore look at Inigo Jones's design for the costume of Iris in Jonson's masque *Hymenaei* (Plate 61), given at the Banqueting House, Whitehall, in 1606, and know that Shakespeare's Iris, in the masque in *The Tempest* six years later, would have worn a very similar dress. As for Ariel, we may suppose that as an airy spirit he would have been dressed in pale blue, or perhaps like the 'Ayrely Sprites' of Inigo Jones's *Temple of Love* designs, who had 'Garments and Caps all of feathers'. In the latter case it will be understood that the association of feathers is with birds and lightness, and thus with airiness by way of its emblems, and not by way of an airy or spiritual appearance. In the same way a Spirit of Air in Somerset's masque in 1613 was dressed in 'a sky-coloured skin-coat with a mantle painted with Fowle and on his head an Eagle'.

The reading of emblems or allegorical 'devices' was closely allied to the

Costume for a Knight Masquer in Lord Hay's Masque, 1607

Elizabethan conception of heraldry as it was presented at the spectacular jousts and 'barriers' which were a feature of Court life. In these the knightly champions, each splendidly armed and caparisoned in his chosen lady's colours, was led into the lists by damsels, and accompanied by a page who explained the meaning of the poetic device and motto on his shield. Thus Sir Henry Lee, a famous champion at these shows, when he was growing old, appeared in a caparison

> . . . charged with crowns
> Oershadowed with a withered running vine
> As who would say "My spring of youth is past".

The atmosphere of this chivalric jousting is intentionally represented by Shakespeare in *Henry V*, where the knights compare horses and armour and comment on the devices of their shields before the morning of Agincourt. It is also echoed closely in two other instances: in the procession of the Greek knights returning from battle in *Troilus and Cressida*, I, ii (for it must be remembered that tales of the heroes of ancient Greece were visualised by the Elizabethans as chivalric romances in the manner of Chaucer's *Palamon and Arcite*), and more closely still in *Pericles*, II, ii, where the knights pass over the stage on the way to the jousting, and as each passes, his squire presents his shield to the Princess Thaisa, who explains the device to her father:

> *Simonides*: What is the fourth?
> *Thaisa*:   A burning torch that's turned upside down
>   The word, *Quod me alit, me extinguit.*
> *Simonides*: Which shows that beauty hath his power and will
>   Which can as well inflame as it can kill.

At the end of the procession comes Pericles himself clad in rusty armour and carrying his own shield, which shows:

> a withered branch, that's only green at top
> The motto, *in hac spe vivo.*
> *Simonides*: A pretty moral:
>   From the dejected state wherein he is,
>   He hopes by you his fortunes yet may flourish.

This mode of romantic chivalry, which was summed up for the Elizabethans in Spenser's *The Faery Queen*, and which, as has just been said, was accepted as the model by which the Elizabethans visualised the heroic Greeks, does not appear to have been similarly accepted by them for the heroic Romans. The general appearance of Roman armour was well known to the Elizabethans, and to some extent they made use of their knowledge on the stage. Plate 40 shows how the Roman style of costume was used side by side with Elizabethan and purely imaginary ones in a performance of *Titus Andronicus* in 1595. But better even than this as a reference to the stage appearance of Roman tragedy, and clearly demonstrating the manner in which it was mixed with both contemporary and chivalric styles, is the series of small insets representing the story of Brutus and Tarquin, with the Rape of Lucrece, as it was presented, probably in dumb-show, in the streets of Amsterdam in 1609 (Plate 26). Notice also in this how the proud tyrant Tarquin bears as his emblems the peacock's feathers of pride and the hammer of tyranny. That he wears a turban is also interesting, since in medieval drama this was the usual way of representing the tyrant Herod. Other pictures of historic and fantastic costumes as the Elizabethans knew them, and in the style in which they were probably used in many cases upon the stage, are shown in Plates 42 and 43. The Speed title-page is particularly worth noting in that it shows an attempt at historical research. I doubt whether a 'Britaine' would ever have appeared in this guise on the stage, but the 'Romane' certainly would, and the fact that two figures in this title page and two others in the Jonson title-page facing it show a distinctive style of loose, open gown, which seems to be associated with the idea of heroic tragedy, indicates that a garment of this kind may also have been commonly used on the stage. In the bottom panel of the Speed design the Norman, although the detail cannot be clearly seen in this reproduction, is wearing long, pointed shoes of a historic medieval type.

Enough has now been said to establish the claim that the Elizabethan theatre, so far from being plain and simple in its appointments, was accustomed to shows of elaborate spectacle against a background ornamented, perhaps very elaborately, in the baroque manner. We may guess, if we will, that much of this was in a garish taste, and perhaps, after all, much of it was 'infantine', as the Victorian writer quoted early in this chapter said it was. It was a mixed bag, in which Hamlet was jostled on either hand by Ralph Roister Doister and Old Hieronimo. It played to the allegorical refinements of courtiers, and to groundlings who, as Hamlet complained, were 'capable of nothing but inexplicable dumb-shows and noise'. Of the dumb-shows we have seen something, and since noise has once already been mentioned as a characteristic feature of the public stage, it would be as well to point out that noise seems to have been enjoyed by the Elizabethan groundling as a pleasure in its own right. The German traveller Paul Hentzner said of Englishmen that they were 'vastly fond of great noises that fill the ear, such as the firing of cannon, drums, and the ringing of bells, so that in London it is common for a number of them that have got a glass in their heads, to go up into some belfry, and ring the bells for hours together for the sake of exercise'. Without taking this report too solemnly it is true that the plays were full, not only of the

F

noise of trumpets and drums, as indeed one might expect, but also of the noise of gunfire which they used on every possible occasion. Shakespeare is full of it. Cannons are shot off not only in battle scenes, but also to give effect to merriment and carouse, as at the feasting of King Claudius in *Hamlet*; and it was the firing of cannon at Cardinal Wolsey's festivities in *Henry VIII* that burned the Globe down in 1613. The acme of all cannonading on the Elizabethan stage was the sea battle, and when in *Antony and Cleopatra* there 'is heard the noise of a sea-fight', that noise was of gunfire from the cannons just outside the theatre. There was at one time a fashion for seafaring plays, largely no doubt because of the rich opportunities for cannonading which they offered. 'The battle at Sea in '88, with England's victory', was to have been one of the attractions of *England's Joy*. And, in *The Silent Woman*, the old curmudgeon Morose, who could bear no noise, being distraught at the uproar which his new wife had brought upon him, named among the noisy penances he would be willing to endure to be rid of her: 'London Bridge, Paris-garden, Billinsgate, when the noises are at their height and loudest. Nay,' he concluded to crown it all, 'Nay, I would sit out a play, that were nothing but fights at sea, drum, trumpet and target.'

6. The Globe Restored

IN ALL this I have tried to steer a course between two opinions of the Globe, the old one that it was a quaint proto-theatre whose rustic limitations might best be allowed to stay where they look so well, in the pages of a picture book; and a new one, that it was a theatre so excellently adapted to bring out all that is best in dramatic art, that its loss was a calamity and its restoration is greatly to be desired. If I must choose between the two I will certainly choose the second, for reasons which will perhaps come better at the end of this chapter than here at the beginning; but I am none the less ready to suspect that if I could be carried back over those three hundred and fifty years and set down among the crowd jostling into the Globe I might, on getting inside, and after my curiosity had abated, find myself perhaps a little more disappointed than I would happily admit, even to myself. But then, it would be quite a while before my curiosity began to abate. To be taken back for one day to the Globe, to see, to verify, to correct and at last to know the truth about this old building is a thing for which William Archer said he would willingly give a year of his life; and I would willingly accompany him upon the same terms, carefully adding, however, as he did, that in bidding for the impossible one can afford to be generous.

That the possibility of disappointment exists is because to have speculated upon the probable facts of the Globe, even for a little while, is to have given play to the historical imagination in a soil so rich, and, moreover, so fertilised by great artists, that the reality even at its best would have much ado to live up to the fantasy that can grow upon it in one's mind. If, therefore, one wishes to re-create the Globe, either by visiting it in imagination or by building a replica of it, upon whatever scale, one ought to be sure what it is that one is setting out to do. I think, for example, that no one would now wish to revive the conditions of the Elizabethan playgoer in the auditorium, any more than one would wish to have, except in a museum, the conditions of the ordinary Elizabethan home and kitchen. What is wished is to restore for certain purposes what I would be careful to distinguish as the *character* of the Elizabethan stage; and even here we should be careful to distinguish again between the character of the facts so far as they can be reconstructed in the light of historical research, and the character of the art, or such of it as we would wish to restore to the life and value of our own use. There is at present still some confusion between these two, so that if a company of actors tries to produce a Shakespearean play in the Elizabethan style, they are liable to be suspected of attempting an arty or antiquarian stunt; while if a historical scholar becomes animated by the living artistic power which lies just under the surface of his research into the Elizabethan theatre, he may, because he feels it all so very much alive, unwittingly translate his findings into modern terms, and transform the valuable dry sticks of historical fact into the bonfire of an enthusiastic but not necessarily accurate personal opinion. In such a way I am tempted at this point to gather together all the themes of this study and use them as sketches from which to rebuild the Elizabethan Globe in the fashion of my own fancy. I would begin by enticing the reader to come with me along a Bankside which looks very like the one we can follow in Hollar's engraving. I think I would like to make it very early in the morning, just in the gloom of dawn. We should only faintly see the clustered boats lying on their sides over there in the mud. The tide would be low. There would be two or three swans palely discernible, drifting downstream. There would be candlelight moving about in a house nearby, and a few lamps showing across the water within the big shadow of the town. At Paris

Garden Stairs, a little way ahead of us, I would have some man, early abroad, hailing a waterman to take him over to the city. His voice echoes. All being so shadowy at this hour, there is nothing, not even the strangeness of a dress, which need be seen clearly enough to puzzle the perception. Not even as it gets lighter, and as, having turned away from the water a short distance down a lane, we arrive at the blank exterior of what seems to be a round building, and which, being set as it is at the loose end of a few houses with some trees near by, reminds us a little of a gas-holder on the outskirts of a country town, not even this at present offers enough detail to dissipate belief. We do not notice what the building is made of, whether of wood or concrete. We notice a door, however. It stands ajar, and creaks a little backwards and forwards in the draught, whilst we are hesitating to go in. The creaking stops, we are relieved to find, as we push it farther open and pass through into a dark and empty yard. We are standing at last within the circle of the Globe. Looking upwards we see the sky grey within the encircling roof. In ten minutes from now, perhaps even less, it will begin to be light enough for us to see clearly at last what we have for so long been trying to imagine. . . .

It is at this moment that I feel a touch on my shoulder, and turning to catch what my companionable reader has to say I find to my surprise that he is no longer with me. Instead there is a figure who, like one of Scrooge's midnight visitors, silently beckons me to follow him. It seems there is a place I must go to in one of the galleries, and as I turn I find—great heavens!— that the galleries are crowded! There they sit in silent rows all around the railings, rustling their note-books and pencils, cleaning and adjusting their spectacles, some wearing eighteenth-century periwigs, some in Victorian high collars, some in nylon shirts and American neckties, some from their graves and some from their beds and some from their seats of learning, all with their books of research around them, and all waiting patiently for it to grow a little lighter. I can just faintly make out one whom I take to be Edmund Malone and there, I see, are J. O. Halliwell-Phillips and W. J. Lawrence, with Sir Edmund Chambers near by. And there are Ashley H. Thorndike, Harley Granville Barker and J. Dover Wilson; and here are Ronald Watkins and Maurice Percival from Harrow, and there again is John Cranford Adams. There sits T. S. Graves with G. F. Reynolds and T. F. Ordish. Richard Southern I recognise, and Allardyce Nicoll; and I think those others must be Karl Gaedertz and Wilhelm Creizenach and Karl Mantzius and Ludwig Tieck, all sitting together. . . . We are eagerly awaiting the light—which this morning is taking longer to come. Meanwhile I think I can just discern, in all the dimness over there across the yard, the shape of the stage buildings just as I have always believed them to have been. Almost certainly the day-light will justify me when it comes. . . . But now there is a suspicion that, like yesterday, it may not come here to-day . . . may not, alas, ever come here again. . . .

❖ ❖ ❖

Perhaps it will be thought that I have laid too much stress upon the uncertainty which partly obscures some portions of this subject. If so it is only because it has seemed to me necessary to redress the balance wherein too much weight has been laid in the other scale, so that details which can be at best only conjectural have often been described as if they were certainties. It is necessary, I think, to hold the matter open as long as possible, so that new theories and fresh interpretations of the evidence can continue to enter in. For example, there have been two studies recently which both indicate a certain routine formality in Elizabethan stage practice, reminding one in some ways of the theatrical conventions of China and Japan. In one [1] Bertram Joseph has pointed out some strong links which he believes connected the art of the Elizabethan actor to the tutored and conventional delivery of the public orator; and in the other [2] Leslie Hotson gives reasons for supposing that the Stage-keepers of the playhouses, who are usually imagined as holding a position more or less equivalent to the modern Stage Manager, were in fact masked attendants, wearing a sort of uniform, who were continually to be seen during a performance, arranging the properties, drawing the curtains when needed (for these were generally drawn by hand, and not as in modern theatres by an invisible cord), and waiting at behest upon those privileged spectators who had seats upon the stage. If these things are true we must again make adjustments to our imagined picture of a performance at the Globe, to give them room.

But whatever details may still be undecided—and even if they have always to remain so—it must not be supposed that the Globe cannot be restored. If we combine all the things that are certain with all the things that can be accepted as more than probable, we can create, if not an exact, at least a characteristically true portrait of the historical Globe. And although there are gaps in the evidence, we can, by studying the material which surrounds the gaps, begin to see evidences of character in the shape of the empty spaces

[1] Bertram L. Joseph, *Elizabethan Acting*.
[2] Leslie Hotson, 'False Faces on Shakespeare's Stage', *T.L.S.*, 16 May, 1952.

themselves—just as an archæologist, finding a small hole in the ground where some object, itself decayed to nothingness, has left its impression moulded in the surrounding earth, will fill this with plaster of paris, and presently recover a complete cast of the original form.

We could, if we wished, rebuild an Elizabethan theatre in some sort of historical form. We could base its general dimensions upon those given in the Fortune and Hope contracts, and thus on a full-size stage, before an audience standing in the yard and sitting in the three tiers of galleries, and with some spectators, if they wished, upon the stage itself, we could give complete performances of Shakespeare's plays in an atmosphere similar to that of their original presentation. Much could be learned and much enjoyed in this; but I fear that an audience that had learned and enjoyed its lesson at one performance might not return for the similar enjoyment of the next. A historical reconstruction in the greatest possible detail and on a large scale is much to be desired; but we should be careful not to confuse such an attractive exhibition-piece with the living artistic reality which still awaits restoration, and to which the historical exhibit is only a background.

The modern proscenium theatre has now reached the limit of its possibilities. Its wide range of visual effects (which is, after all, the characteristic which it has chosen to develop above all others) has been supplemented by that of the cinema, and this again will soon be increased by the range of the three-dimensional colour-movie. All this, which has now become a special sort of theatre, conceived more and more in terms of dramatic pictures, has now been brought to our very firesides by television, which again is likely to increase the range of its effects so widely, that one may suppose the whole capacity of drama from the visual point of view is soon to be complete. And yet the more this side of the theatre develops, the more noticeable it becomes that one whole section of the theatrical scale is being left out, simply because it is incompatible with the production of this kind of effect. For instance, it is well known that the cinema, for all its wealth of technical accomplishment, is quite unable to do justice to the simple picture of an orchestra of any size playing anything at all, be it the *Tannhäuser* Overture or *Three Blind Mice*. A purely musical event is simply not cinema material. Neither is ballet. Not all the cunning of colour photography nor of changeable camera angles is able to disguise the fact that, to enjoy a ballet, it is necessary to be sitting personally in view of the actual dancers, to see all their movements relative to the whole fixed space of the floor they are dancing upon; and, above all, to know that one is seeing a complete, unique and *unedited* display of an ephemeral art. The fact of an aesthetic magnetism between a performer and his audience is too well known to need re-emphasising here, but what may need to be pointed out is that with each step of development in the progress of the more visual side of drama, a little of this personal magnetism has had to be sacrificed. There is no likelihood, nor any reason to wish, that the technique of the visually specialised theatre (in the widest sense of the word) will be discontinued or even modified. But it seems now that the time is ripe to develop that other type of theatre which is not so much concerned with the scenic effect of a whole stage, as it is with the direct experience of that sort of artistic enchantment by which actors can create an imaginary world upon an empty space. For this the ideal stage is one in which the actors can come out into a close relation with their audience, standing, only a little separated, in the midst of them, as they did in Shakespeare's time. There is nothing thin or meagre or colourless about this form of art, unless art itself is colourless or meagre or thin. Only it should not be compared for its effect with the effects of the picture stage, any more than sculpture should be compared with painting. It is a different thing, and seeks to provide a different sort of experience. The full range of its capacities we can hardly tell as yet, because, after the neglect of three hundred years, this form of theatre is only just beginning to be used again; and in order to take it up where it was left off, it is being used at present mainly for revivals of Shakespeare. But if, in restoring the type of the great Shakespearean stage, the impression is given that it is being done out of a spirit of antiquarian research or else in order to provide some quaint occasional novelty, it will be great damage to a good cause. For on such a stage one might now hope to see the development of an intelligent dramatic form in which the work of individual artists can be enjoyed as a concert is enjoyed, in a clear and concentrated space. To wish for such a thing is not an antiquarianism; neither is it a sort of fad, to be suspected of suggesting that the 'picture-frame stage' is obsolete and needs to be superseded by the 'platform stage'. Both of these stages are desirable; but only one, the proscenium stage, is at present generally available. It is only as a first step towards developing all the potential richness of the other that I suggest it is now high time we had the Globe restored.

Notes on the
Illustrations

NOTES ON THE ILLUSTRATIONS

SECTION I. THE LONDON THEATRES

Plate 1 LONDON FROM BANKSIDE, SHOWING THE GLOBE AND THE BEAR-GARDEN, *c.* 1616. From the engraving by J. C. Visscher

Visscher's panorama of London, of which this is a part, was published in Amsterdam in 1616, but the precise date and nature of the information upon which it was founded is uncertain. It is not considered likely that the engraver worked from first-hand knowledge of London, but rather that he drew from previous maps and views, perhaps supplemented by sketches and verbal information from eyewitnesses. But from the evidence at his disposal, whatever it may have been, he was clearly satisfied that the Globe was a polygonal building. At the time of the first publication of the print this would have been the second Globe, which was erected in 1614; but this does not exclude a possibility that the engraver might have worked on out-of-date information referring to the first Globe.

Guildhall Library, London

Plate 2 BANKSIDE, SHOWING THE PLAYHOUSES, 1600. From a revised version of John Norden's earlier (1593) map of London

91

This rare representation of Bankside was described by I. A. Shapiro in an article in *Shakespeare Survey I* in 1948. Since then the accuracy which Mr. Shapiro claimed for it has been confirmed by the discovery of other evidence which is published in the Bankside volume (Volume 22) of the *Survey of London*. The Norden Map reproduced here is the only one which shows the playhouses correctly placed in relation to one another, but it should be noted that the Rose is misnamed as the Star.

Reproduced from the Civitas Londini *map in the Royal Library, Stockholm*

Plate 3 AIR VIEW OF BANKSIDE, 1949

The sites of three of the theatres are ringed. The fourth, the Swan, which is shown in the Norden map (Plate 2) lies off to the left, outside the range of this photograph. Sketch map, herewith, shows modern street names.

(*Note:* The white area beside Cannon Street Station, and the transparency of the station roof are the result of bomb damage in 1940.)

Plate 4 BANKSIDE SHOWING THE THEATRES (with their names reversed) SHORTLY BEFORE 1644. From the engraving by Wenzel Hollar

Hollar's complete panorama of London, of which this is the western portion, is the most convincing of all the views of the City before the Great Fire. Much, if not all, of it is based upon sketches made by Hollar from the tower of Southwark Cathedral (cf. Plate 5), and is therefore known to have the general authority of an eyewitness account. It does not follow, however, that it is to be trusted in all details, since the engraving was made not in London but in Antwerp, where it was first published in 1647. Because of his Royalist sympathies, Hollar had been forced to leave London in 1644—incidentally the year in which the second Globe was demolished. He took his sketches with him, but to supplement these and to refresh his memory of some of the details he seems to have used the well-known (and presumably approved) Visscher panorama (Plate 1). In particular, he has followed Visscher in naming the Bear-garden and the Globe from left to right in that order, thereby in fact confusing them. This confusion of names is fully dealt with in the article by I. A. Shapiro, and in Volume 22 of the *Survey of London* referred to in the note to Plate 2, above.

Note on the far side of the river, between Blackfriars and Baynards Castle, a long roof which may be the roof of Blackfriars Hall, which had been made into a Private Theatre in Queen Elizabeth's time, and was occupied by the King's Men (Shakespeare's company) from 1608 onwards. Farther to the left Arundel House is marked by the waterside. Here Hollar himself lived and worked under the patronage of the Earl of Arundel.

British Museum

Plate 5 ORIGINAL DRAWING OF THE SECOND GLOBE AND THE BEAR-GARDEN by Wenzel Hollar

This, a detail from a larger drawing of Bankside, is here reproduced the same size as the original. It is in pencil, partly traced over in ink. It is to be presumed, though it is not certain, that the inking-over was also by Hollar's hand, though there is reason to suspect that this was done later than the pencil drawing. There are some small and interesting differences between this drawing and the plate (Plate 4) which was engraved from it. For instance, the drawing shows the Bear-garden (right) as appearing a little smaller than the Globe, which was probably due to the effect of perspective, since the Bear-garden was farther away from the spectator. In the engraving, however, this disparity has been 'corrected', an effect which is apt to happen unconsciously in details of this kind when copying from one drawing to another. It is also interesting to note, as I. A. Shapiro points out (*Shakespeare Survey II*, p. 21), that the flagpole of the Bear-garden (right), which in the engraving is shown thrusting up as from the middle of the arena, appears in the drawing (where it is only faintly marked) to stand not inside but on the *outside* wall of the building, and just about where the far-side staircase-housing should be. In the same way, above the right-hand staircase of the Globe (left) there is a tall thing inked in, which, as Shapiro says, hardly seems likely for a chimney and may have been drawn originally as a flagpole.

It should be noted particularly that Hollar's representations of the play-houses are the only ones which show these buildings in what are known to be their correct proportions. All other exterior views of them show them as being much too tall and narrow. The question as to whether they were also round, as Hollar shows them, or whether for convenience of drawing he has simplified a polygon, can perhaps never now be decided. Lastly, and with reference to the confusion in the names of these two playhouses (see Note to Plate 4 above), it will be noted that the names were not indicated at all in this sketch, and Hollar, working from it in Antwerp, had to rely upon his memory to tell him which was which.

Collection of Iolo A. Williams Esq.

Plate 6 BANKSIDE. Detail from the *Civitas Londini* view.

This is a recently discovered view, and is to some extent based upon the Norden map shown in Plate 2. Both in fact were included in the same large view of London now in the Royal Library, Stockholm.

Royal Library, Stockholm

Plate 7 THE SWAN THEATRE, *c.* 1596

This famous drawing, often referred to as 'the de Witt sketch', is not in fact in the hand of its originator, Johannes de Witt, but of his friend Arend van Buchel of Utrecht. De Witt had visited London in or about 1596, and a letter from him describing the Swan theatre was copied by van Buchel in-to a commonplace book, together with this drawing. It may therefore be presumed that the drawing also was copied from an original by de Witt, but of course we cannot be sure whether or by how much van Bu-chel has altered it in the copying. However, it remains the only contem-porary picture of the interior of an Elizabethan playhouse, and its value as evidence is corroborated by the many points (the 'Heavens', the flag, the pillars on the stage, the three tiers of galleries, etc.) in which it tallies with other independent evidence.

The notes on the drawing were put in to point the comparison with the Roman theatre which de Witt mentions in his letter. The appropriate part of the Latin text is given in translation below:

'There are in London four theatres [amphitheatra] of noteworthy beauty, which bear diverse names according to their diverse signs. In them a different action [varia scaena] is daily presented to the people. The two finest of these are situated to the southward beyond the Thames, named, from the signs they display, the Rose and the Swan. Two others are outside the city towards the north, and are approached "per Episcopalem portem"; in the vernacular, "Biscopgate". There is also a fifth, of dissimilar structure, devoted to beast-baiting, wherein many bears, bulls, and dogs of stupendous size are kept in separate dens and cages, which, being pitted against each other, afford men a most delightful [jucundissimum] spectacle. Of all the theatres, however, the largest and most distinguished is that whereof the sign is a swan (commonly called the Swan theatre), since it has space for three thousand persons, and is built of a concrete of flint stones (which greatly abound in Britain) and supported by wooden columns, painted in such excellent imitation of marble that it might deceive even the most prying [nasutissimos]. Since its form seems to approach that of a Roman structure, I have depicted it above.'

Plates 8 & 9 DEBASED VERSIONS OF THE GLOBE, EIGHTEENTH CENTURY

Copied, probably at several removes, from originals already incorrect in themselves, such engravings as these served to puzzle the early Shakespearean investigators. The view on the left, dating probably from the first half of the eighteenth century, is believed to be an Italian copy deriving originally from an engraving by Merian first published in Frankfort in 1638. Merian himself probably took most of his material from Visscher (Plate 1). Visscher is the original of our other view (right), which was published in London in 1789.

Plate 10 AN EARLY ATTEMPT AT RECONSTRUCTION

This mid-Victorian water-colour by George Pycroft was in its time a reasonable attempt to make sense out of the material then available. The Swan drawing and the Fortune and Hope contracts, with their express statements of three tiers of galleries, could not have been known to the artist, though he seems to have had some knowledge of Renaissance theatrical engravings, for he shows a high stage in the typical manner of the early street theatres. His idea of the Heavens seems to be based upon Malone's incorrect notion that 'pieces of drapery tinged with blue' might have been 'suspended across the stage to represent the heavens'. It was a shot in the dark, guided by a knowledge of the ordinary proscenium stage's use of sky borders. Accordingly, Pycroft's drawing shows a piece of drapery suspended on curtain rings across the stage. In front of this hangs a notice indicating the scene, a 'Plain near Shrewsbury'. This, a common fallacy in Pycroft's time, and one which is still sometimes credited, derives from a misunderstanding of the Elizabethan use of title boards. The nineteenth-century scholars supposed, seeing that no scenic illusion could be offered on the Elizabethan stage, that it must have been necessary to supply the want in some visual way; it seems not to have occurred to them that Shakespeare's plays, if played as written (which the Victorians did not do), automatically explain their own supposed localities as they go along. The extent of the Elizabethan use of title boards may be disputable, especially so far as the public theatres were concerned, but it is clear enough that they were not used to show individual scenes, but were supposed to indicate localities to be accepted more or less permanently throughout the play. Thus several doors would be marked each with the name of the person or place with which it was to be specially associated (cf. Plate 15). This was, of course, a variation of the medieval use of 'mansions', but although Elizabethan critics tended to frown upon its absurdities ('What Child is there', writes Sir Philip Sidney, 'that coming to a Play, and seeing *Thebes* written in great letters upon an old door, doth believe that it is Thebes?') Elizabethan actors seem to have found it too useful to dispense with altogether. It seems also to have been customary at times (though again the extent of the practice is very questionable, and it may have referred principally to private performances) to hang up a board inscribed with the title of the play. It will be noted that Pycroft shows labels over all the entrances in the proper manner.

Pycroft's sign on the theatre wall seems, like his Heavens, to be based on Malone, who reported from William Oldys (1696–1761) that the Globe displayed for a sign 'a figure of Hercules supporting the Globe, under which was written *Totus mundus agit histrionem*'. Such a sign would, however, have been hung outside rather than within the theatre.

For all its shortcomings, the picture has many merits, perhaps not the least being that it demonstrates the discomfiture that waits upon even the best intending of historical reconstructions in the end.

Picture Post Library

Plate 11 THE GLOBE: A RECONSTRUCTION OF 1910

I have chosen this reconstruction by A. Forestier which appeared in the *Illustrated London News* in 1910, because it sums up very well the attitude of the most informed opinion at that time about the conditions of the Elizabethan playhouses, and indeed in many respects it is the opinion still popularly held to-day. Forestier was an artist who specialised in historical reconstructions, and it is difficult not to feel convinced by such an excellent example of his work as this. None the less, although the hurly-burly atmosphere of the auditorium is very well expressed (and it is typical of the date of this reconstruction that it should approach the subject so much from the picturesque point of view) the details of the stage background itself are imaginary, and are drawn not from original sources but from the deductions of nineteenth-century scholars and editors. In its general appearance the drawing is, of course, founded upon the de Witt sketch (Plate 7) but the addition of a curtained 'inner stage' and the angled setting of the side doors and windows are ideas which de Witt does not support. The attempt, in such reconstructions, to provide a sort of enclosed space at the rear of the stage derives, I suspect, more from a wish in the nineteenth-century mind to equate the Elizabethan stage with some at least of the habitual practices of the familiar nineteenth-century proscenium stage than from any evidence the Elizabethan stage itself has to offer. Other things which may be assumed to be incorrect in this drawing are the upper building over the stage (which was almost certainly built forward, overhanging the stage, so that the heavenly throne could descend on to the stage, in front of the background façade); and the rather plain appearance of the whole stage presentation—a typical Elizabethan play and playhouse is likely to have been decked out in a more florid and showy fashion than this.

Illustrated London News

Plate 12 AN OPENING FROM HENSLOWE'S DIARY FOR 1597–98

If Philip Henslowe's name is remembered as second to the Burbages in the theatrical fame of his time, it is perhaps only because he did not have the good fortune to be much associated with Shakespeare. He was the most enterprising manager of theatrical affairs of his day. He owned at one time or another the Rose, the Fortune and the Hope theatres, and one other at Newington Butts. His son-in-law was Edward Alleyn, the great rival in fame of Richard Burbage. A famous collection of private papers belonging to Henslowe and Alleyn has been handed down in the muniment of Dulwich College, the College of God's Gift which Alleyn founded and opened in 1617. The most famous of these documents is

Henslowe's so-called 'diary', really an account and memorandum book. The opening from it shown in this plate is reprinted in clear with explanatory notes at Appendix C.

Reproduced by permission of the Governors of Dulwich College

Plate 13 PORTION OF A LETTER FROM EDWARD ALLEYN TO HIS WIFE

The letter was written during the great plague of 1593 when, the London theatres being closed, the players were touring the provinces. It was written from Bristol on August 1st. The whole text is as follows (the portion shown in the plate being indicated in the margin):

'Emmanuel,
'My good sweet Mouse,
'I commend me heartily to you and to my father, my mother, and my sister Bess, hoping in God though the sickness be round about you yet, by His Mercy, it may excape your house, which, by the grace of God, it shall. Therefore use this course; keep your house fair and clean, which I know you will, and every evening throw water before your door, and in your backside, and have in your windows good store of rue and herb of grace, and with all the grace of God, which must be obtained by prayers; and so doing, no doubt but the Lord will mercifully defend you.

'Now, good mouse, I have no news to send you but this, that we have all our health, for which the Lord be praised. I received your letter at Bristow, by Richard Cowley, for the which I thank you.

'I have sent you by this bearer, Thomas Pope's kinsman, my white waistcoat, because it is a trouble to me to carry it. Receive it with this letter, and lay it up for me till I come.

'If you send any more letters, send to me by the carriers of Shrewsbury or to West Chester or to York, to be kept till my Lord Strange's players come.

'And thus, sweetheart, with my hearty commentations to all our friends, I cease from Bristow this Wednesday after Saint James his day, being ready to begin the play of *Harry of Cornwall*.

'Mouse, do my hearty commends to Mr. Grigs' wife and all his household, and to my sister Phillips.

'Your Loving husband,
'E. Alleyn.'

'Mouse, you send me no news of any things you should send of your domestical matters; such things as happen at home, as how your distilled water proves, or this, or that, or any thing what you will.

'And Jug, I pray you let my orange tawny stockings of woollen be dyed a very good black against I come home to wear in the winter.

'You sent me not word of my garden, but next time you will. But remember this, in any case, that all that bed which was parsley in the month of September, you sow it with spinach, for then is the time. I would do it myself but we shall not come home till Allholland tide. And so, sweet mouse, farewell, and brook our long journey with patience.'

Reproduced by permission of the Governors of Dulwich College

Plate 14 'THE PLATT OF THE SECOND PART OF THE SEVEN DEADLY SINS'

The 'Platt' or Plot of a play was (as here shown) a synopsis of the action. It appears to have been customary to have the 'Platt' mounted on a board and hung up within the tiring-house for quick reference by the back-stage staff during the course of a play: for it should be remembered that plays were only given for two or three days at a time at the outside, or even for single performances only, and not for runs as nowadays; so that it would be necessary for the back-stage organisation to have some quick reference at hand for the prompt marshalling of costumes, properties, etc. The present example (which is reprinted for easier reference at Appendix D) was found pasted into the covers of a book, to serve as an end paper, and the dark mark across the middle is the spine of the book-cover. The rectangular mark in the middle of the upper half is a hole in the paper, believed to be the hole where the platt-board was originally hung upon a peg in the tiring-house.

The play itself is a Morality, indicating by seven legendary examples the effects of the Deadly Sins. The First Part, which is lost, evidently dealt with the first four of the sins. In the Second, as is shown in the first item of the Platt, all seven sins take the stage together, but the last three drive in the other four (who have already had their turn) and then proceed to present their own examples. Two saintly characters, the monk Lidgate and King Henry VI, comment upon the action from time to time.

A feature of particular interest is that the actors of the play are referred to sometimes in the characters they personate and sometimes by their own names, e.g.: 'Enter King Gorboduk . . . R. Burbadge, Mr. Brian, Th. Goodale. The Queen with Ferrex & Porrex and some attendants . . .'

From the knowledge thus gained it appears that this Platt refers to a production given by a company which was occupying Henslowe's Rose around 1591–92. This must therefore have been a revival, for the author, Richard Tarlton the great comedian, had died in 1588.

Reproduced by permission of the Governors of Dulwich College

SECTION II. STREET THEATRES

Plate 15 THE STAGE FOR 'LAURENTIUS', COLOGNE, 1581

This unique drawing shows an open-air stage erected for a play dealing with the martyrdom of St. Lawrence. The scenic arrangements are carefully annotated, and it would seem that this sketch is either an original design for the stage layout, or else (perhaps more likely) a record of a successful arrangement noted for use on future occasions. The method of presentation is recognisably medieval: but it is also similar to much Elizabethan practice in England, especially during the earlier period. But the method, as I have noted elsewhere in the text, was probably maintained in part even into Jacobean times; and indeed the atmosphere of this martyrdom play seems very similar to that of Massinger's *The Virgin Martyr* (which may be conjectured as having been acted around 1614, that is to say a date midway between 1606, when Massinger left college, and 1622, when the play was first printed). It may be noted that when this *Laurentius* stage was erected in Cologne, the early public theatres of Burbage and Henslowe had already been in business for five years.

The *Laurentius* stage is shown as having been built around two standing trees, which may remind us of the two pillars in the de Witt drawing. The stage is supported on barrels, and its planks appear to be strewn with something, perhaps sand or earth, making pathway areas upon it; perhaps this was to deaden the noise of feet on the stage. Around the stage the old medieval 'houses' are represented by their doors (cf. note to Plate 10). The 'houses', from left to right, are allotted to the High Priest of Jupiter, to Augustus and Valerianus; then comes the Praetorium, and two thrones for Augustus and the Praetor; then the plinth of a statue, of which more is to be said below; next, the house of Hippolitus; then a prison; then the houses of Sixtus and Faustina; then an odd corner which seems to have been ramped up to represent a hill, the Caelian Mount; and on the right a door representing the ancient gate of Rome, Porta Capena.

In the forefront left and right are the idolatrous monuments to which St. Lawrence refused tribute; on the left, upon the altar of Jove, the oil and wine which he would not pour stand ready by the sacred flame. The object towards the right centre is the gridiron upon which the saint was roasted.

Returning to the central plinth, this is marked as 'Locus statuae SS martyris Laurentii': 'the place for the statue of the most holy martyr Lawrence'. The curious thing is that this plinth is not built out on to the stage as other things are, but is painted on the scenic wall. It gives me to suppose that the actual standing-place for the statue was in the rear, behind the scenic wall, and that the part above the plinth was covered throughout the play with a curtain painted like the rest of the wall. At the end of the play, however, one must suppose that a statue of the martyred saint was exposed here, as in a niche, the curtain being then drawn aside; and it would be reasonable to think that the actor who had personated the saint would have taken his place here as the statue, behind the curtain. To complete the conjecture, it was probably a miraculous statue that moved and spoke.

Photo: Oskar Fischel Collection

Plate 16 A FLEMISH STREET THEATRE, *c.* 1650

Apparently a medicine show, with comedians in the Italian style. Note the canopy over the stage, which harks back to the idea of the 'shadow or cover', as at the Fortune. The sketch is by Jakob van der Ulft (1627–88).

From Monumenta Scenica

Plate 17 A MOUNTEBANK STAGE, *c.* 1600

An outdoor stage in its most primitive form, the nucleus and beginning of all stages. Note the height of it, which is characteristic. The actors are Italian comedians, selling medicines (shown on the table at left).

British Museum

Plate 18 A STREET THEATRE IN LOUVAIN, 1594

Primitive forms of street booth stages are shown in Plates 22 and 23, and on p. ix. The booth here is interesting because it shows the next stage of development, i.e., ornamentation by painted fascias. Note trestles.

This drawing is a nineteenth-century lithographic copy (by Edward van Even) of a sixteenth-century drawing which was destroyed in the burning of Louvain library in 1914. Mr. George R. Kernodle, from whose book *From Art to Theatre* this is taken, informs me that the buildings in the background were added by van Even, who says there was no background to the original which he copied.

The play is the *Judgement of Solomon*.

Kernodle: From Art to Theatre

Plate 19 CHRIST SHOWN TO THE PEOPLE. Etching (1st state) by Rembrandt, 1655

There is good reason to suppose that this composition by Rembrandt is based upon a theatrical show seen and sketched by him in a Flemish street. The central structure has a marked resemblance to the Rederyker stages of the type shown in Plates 21, 27 and 28: the empty space on the upper level was probably originally an upper stage covered with a curtain. With a little imagination it is possible to see in this picture something of the appearance of a play in an Elizabethan inn-yard, or even perhaps something suggestive of a performance in Henslowe's square-built theatre, the Fortune (though the stage of the Fortune was much larger).

British Museum

Plate 20 STAGE IN BRUSSELS, 1594

A Throne of Honour, attended by Virtues and Angels of Fame.

From Kernodle: From Art to Theatre

Plate 21 FLEMISH STREET THEATRE, 1607

Note trestles supporting the stage.

Photo: Oskar Fischel Collection

Plate 22 BASQUE FOLK-DANCE STAGE, *c.* 1934

This stage, photographed by the late Rodney Gallop at Tardets in the Pyrenees, shows an ancient and traditional form of theatre still in use. Note especially (and compare with Plate 21 above) the trestled stage, the curtained booth and the centrally placed upper stage which is occupied by musicians.

The dance here in progress was described by Mr. Rodney Gallop (in the *Geographical Magazine* for July, 1935) as being dramatic in form, the action taking place between 'Christians' and 'Turks'. The 'Christians' hold the stage, and some of the 'Turks' are on horseback in front of it.

The following extract will also be of interest. It is from 'The Place of

Rhythm in the Basque Pastorales', by Violet Alsford (*Journal of the English Folk Dance and Song Society*, Volume VII, No. 1, December 1952):

'The village people go to great expense when they decide to perform their play. The stage is of planks laid on barrels,[1] towering tiers of wooden seats are built up. . . . The backcloth is of beautifully-arranged white sheets lightly decorated in the tasteful manner of this people, with small green garlands swaying in the spring air. The traditional *tchirulari*, playing the three-holed pipe and the long, stringed drum, sits at the back of the stage. Other musicians (clarinet, brass, small drum) sit in an arbour constructed high above the backcloth. Below, two doors lead *on* to, not off from the stage and when actors enter, in the language of the theatre, they "go out" in the language of the Pastorale. This arrangement comes directly from the "mansions" of the Mystery plays. Over the left-hand door are blue flowers, over the right-hand one red, and an Idol or Mahoma is fixed above the red one. This is a polichinelle figure with horns, partaking of the Devil and the supposed God of the Moors. . . . Sometimes there is a central door of gold and white for the use of Angels, Bishops, the lesser clergy, and the dead who enter Paradise through it.

'The "ladies" follow the fashion in their costumes and have done so for at least eighty years since they were in crinolines. In 1951 the Bride of Robert le Diable wore an elegant white dress made by the village dressmaker, with a wreath and veil from the Bon Marché of Bayonne . . . .'.

Photo: Paul Popper

Plate 23 ENGLISH STREET THEATRE AND PLAYERS, 1676

Here again is the traditional high-standing stage with the little booth at the back. It is no different in its essential form from another English example of the same period, the famous frontispiece to Kirkman's *The Wits* (page 39), though in the latter case the stage has been adapted for use indoors.

Photo: Common Ground Ltd.

SECTION III. PAGEANTS AND CELEBRATIONS

Plates 24 & 25 TWO DETAILS FROM 'THE TRIUMPH OF ISABELLA', 1615

The large painting by Denis van Alsloot from which these two details were taken is in the Victoria and Albert Museum, London, and shows a

[1] Cf. Plate 15.

procession of ten splendid cars in the Baroque style winding through the Grande Place in Brussels. The procession was an annual one, but on the occasion shown here it was given with particular splendour in honour of the Archduchess Isabella of the Netherlands, who had distinguished herself a few days previously with the crossbow at a ceremonial shooting match given by the Guild of Crossbowmen, the senior Guild in charge of this procession. The Archduchess herself rode in the procession, and hers is the car shown in the foreground of Plate 25. She is attended by the ladies of her court, and Fame sits before her on a pillar, sounding upon two trumpets (cf. Plate 45). Other cars partly seen in the background carry tableaux of the Annunciation (left) and the Stem of Jesse (right). The principal car in Plate 24 presents a tableau of the Nativity, attended by peasants. In the background is one of a fantastic file of processional monsters.

I include these pictures within my subject principally to show the rich style in which an essentially theatrical display was decorated at that time. Note especially the fine painted hangings. In the Nativity group it is of interest to note how elaborate Corinthian columns have been combined with a thatched roof. If the stage roof at the first Globe was thatched (like the rest of that theatre), it might be supposed to have been supported on similar columns (as in the Swan drawing, q.v.) and the effect would have been something like what we see here.

Crown Copyright reserved　　　　　　　　　　　*Victoria and Albert Museum*

Plate 26　THE TARQUIN STAGE, AMSTERDAM, 1609

The occasion of this show, which was given in Amsterdam on May 5th, 1609, by the Love-in-Bloom Rhetoric (Rederyker) Society, was the signing in the previous month of the Twelve Years' Truce which ended the long Dutch war with Spain. The appropriate subject chosen for this performance was the expulsion of the Tarquins from Rome. This record of it was engraved by J. C. Visscher after a drawing by Verschuring, and is quite unique as a record of any theatrical entertainment of the time, since the staging of each incident is shown in detail. There is one important factor, however, in which it differs from the more typical theatres of its period: it is a picture-frame stage. The reason for this is that it was not a play in the usual sense, but rather a series of short posed episodes, 'tableaux vivants', linked, presumably, by a descriptive recitation from the man who appears before the curtain in the central panel of the engraving.

That the show was given in *tableau vivant* style is demonstrated not only by the picture-frame form of the stage itself, which we have just noted, but also by the staging of episode 9, in the bottom left corner. Obviously this episode can only have been staged by the use of one or perhaps two dummies, and the possibility of live action (if there was any action at all) was limited to the short time required for the striking off of two dummy heads, followed perhaps by some moralising upon the general effect. The *tableau vivant* idea is also supported by the fact that in several of the views the hands of the curtain-drawers can be seen, which, with the temporary way in which the curtains appear to be held back, strongly suggests that each episode was only shown for a short while. In character and action the whole performance recalls the dumb-shows of Elizabethan drama.

The episodes, which read always from left to right across the spread, are as follows: (1) Tarquin is shown in the symbolical action of striking down the tallest flowers of the land. (2) Another symbolic group which shows Tarquin treading the nobility of Rome under foot. Brutus, however, raises his head. (3) The Roman nobles visit the Delphic oracle, who pronounces that he among them who first kisses his own mother shall be the deliverer of Rome from the tyrant. Brutus at once kisses Mother Earth. (4) Meanwhile Sextus, son of Tarquin, violates Lucretia, wife of Collatinus. (5) Lucretia announces her intention of wiping out the stain on her honour by killing herself. (This certainly suggests a speech by Lucretia.) (6) Lucretia stabs herself. Brutus and Collatinus vow vengeance. (7) The Tarquins are driven out. (8) The two sons of Brutus plot with Tarquin and Sextus to restore them to the kingdom. Note how simple is the method adopted to show the eavesdropper, through whom the plot is reported to Brutus. (9) Brutus, putting the security of the State above family, orders the execution of his sons. On the English stage at this time the actors would not have spared pains to make a dummy which would spurt real blood. Maybe the same was done in this case. (10) The freedom of the new Roman Republic, like the month-old Dutch Republic of 1609, is established and guarded by its heroes.

From Monumenta Scenica

Plate 27 REDERYKER STAGE AT ANTWERP, 1582

One of a series erected for the ceremonial welcome of Francis of Anjou, Duke of Brabant. Others of this series of stages were built to a similar pattern, having, like this one, a large upper stage on which biblical tableaux were presented, and a lower stage enclosing an allegorical figure: in this instance a Fury or Vice is seen locked in the dungeon of Hell.

From Monumenta Scenica

Plate 28 STREET THEATRE, GHENT, 1539

Another example of the ornate Rederyker stage. It will be observed that this florid Baroque style of theatre architecture was well established in the Netherlands as early as 1539.

Plate 29 THE TRIUMPH OF JAMES I, LONDON, 1604: (1) The Flemish Arch

That many of the foregoing examples are Flemish and not English may be argued against their acceptance as evidence for the style of the Elizabethan theatre. But our next six examples which were built in the streets of London for the Coronation Procession of James I are English; and if they are not strictly theatres, they are theatrical in character, construction, and use. This and its neighbour may be compared with the two Flemish examples opposite, when it will be seen that there is nothing to choose between them in point of style and ornament. As a useful link between the English and Flemish examples, this (Plate 29) shows the Flemish offering to the London celebrations. It features James I in his Imperial robes. Beneath him are figures representing the seventeen provinces of Flanders. Other figures represent political emblems. Surmounting the whole is a figure of Divine Providence.

British Museum

Plate 30 THE TRIUMPH OF JAMES I, 1604: (2) The Temple of Janus

The theme of this arch, which stood at Temple Bar, was devised by Ben Jonson. Its central feature, immediately over the arch, was a tableau in which a figure representing the Genius of the City of London (right), after a dialogue with a Roman Flamen, sacrificed the heart of the City to James. The part of the Genius of the City was spoken by the actor Edward Alleyn. In the niche above is the figure of Peace, with War grovelling at her feet. The other niches hold figures of Quiet, Safety, Felicity, and Liberty, trampling upon Tumult, Danger, Unhappiness, and Servitude respectively.

Stephen Harrison, who was not only the artist responsible for the engraving of these plates, but also the architect who built the arches themselves, tells us that the walls and gates of this arch were made to resemble brass, the pillars silver, with gold capitals and bases.

British Museum

Plate 31 THE TRIUMPH OF JAMES I, 1604: (3) The Arch of London

This arch, devised by Ben Jonson, stood in Fenchurch Street, where James began his procession. As he approached, a silk curtain painted to represent a cloud, which was spread across the top part of the arch, dropped, and revealed the panorama of London which we see. At the same time the 'waites and hault-boyes of the City', seen in the openings on each side, began to play, and the Genius of the City (personified by Edward Alleyn) began his speech of welcome. He is seen in the central niche, his arm raised. On either side of him stand figures of the Wisdom and Warlike Strength of the City. Above him, on the highest throne, sits Monarchia Britannia, with, on the lesser thrones beneath her, Gladness, Loving Affection, Unanimity, Promptitude and Vigilance. The Genius of the City rouses old Thames, who is shown asleep on the pedestal below, and he also speaks his welcome before the King passes through on his way to the next arch.

British Museum

Plate 32 THE TRIUMPH OF JAMES I, 1604: (4) The Garden of Plenty

This magnificent arbour, at which the King arrived midway in his procession and where he stopped to refresh himself, 'seemed to grow' close to the little Conduit in Cheapside, which 'served as a Fountain to water the Fruits of Plenty. . . . The roof and sides of these Gates were hung with Pompions, Cowcumbers, Grapes, Cherries, Peares, Apples and all other fruits which the land bringeth forth.' The round tops were 'garnished with lesser fruits and all sorts of flowers made by Art'. On the summit of the structure stood Fortune. In the niche below were Peace and Plenty; and below them again Gold and Silver supporting the Globe of the World, with Pomona and Ceres on each side. In the openings above the archways sat the Nine Muses (left), and the Seven Liberal Sciences (right). The King, as he approached, was met by 'Sylvanus and his followers, who, upon sight of his Majesty, played upon Cornets' and escorted him to a room above, where refreshment awaited him.

British Museum

Plate 33 THE TRIUMPH OF JAMES I, 1604 : (5) The New Arabia Felix

Thomas Dekker was responsible for this conception. The Arabia Felix of the title signified the happy land of Britain. As James drew near, Fame, in the topmost alcove, blew her trumpet, whereupon the personages in the large opening below awoke as from sleep and the fountain in the centre (The Fount of Virtue) 'ran wine very plenteously'. The figures of the display represented the Five Senses 'upon five green mounts', with reclining in the foreground, Oblivion and Detraction. These, when the trumpet wakened them, tried to break down the Fount of Virtue with clubs, but the Five Senses prevented them. Once again, as in Plate 31, we see the musicians in the galleries at the sides.

Thirty feet in front of this arch there was a stage set up, 'railed round about with pilasters', upon which verses were recited by a number of allegorical personages.

British Museum

Plate 34 THE TRIUMPH OF JAMES I, 1604 : (6) The Arch of the New World

In the centre of this Baroque fantasy (for which Thomas Middleton was in part responsible) is a great Globe 'filled with all the estates that are in the land'. Upon it stands Fortune, and around it stand the Four Elements, Fire, Air, Earth and Water, who kept it turning like a wheel. Harrison says the Elements 'were placed so quaintly that the Globe seemed to have his motion even on the Crowns of their heads'. Among the twenty-three figures of this display, described as 'lively garnishments', were The Four Cardinal Virtues (Justice, Fortitude, Temperance, and Prudence) enclosed on the (spectator's) right of the Globe, and the four Kingdoms of England, Scotland, Ireland and France, on the left. Perhaps in this case only the Four Elements were living persons, the rest being either paintings or effigies.

British Museum

Plate 35 THE CHARIOT OF ROYAL JUSTICE

An engraving of the early seventeenth century (from a drawing by Martin de Vos) which illustrates not only the design of a processional car, with an outdoor stage (in background), but also the fashionable taste in allegory. A king, attended by Wisdom and Justice, is drawn by the two horses of Rewards and Punishments—these being the theme also represented by the tableaux on the stage.

Plate 36 THE ELVETHAM ENTERTAINMENT FOR QUEEN ELIZABETH I, 1591

An eighteenth-century engraving copied from a contemporary original. The Queen was entertained at Elvetham, in Hampshire, by the Earl of Hertford. For the spectacle shown here this crescent-shaped lake had been specially made, and, because his own house was too small for the Queen and her Court, he had built a state room and other buildings for her in the park. These are shown at the top of the picture.

In the lake were a 'Ship Isle' (D), whose masts turned into trees (presumably the three flagged columns in this engraving represent masts); a Fort, given by Neptune for the protection of the Queen; and a 'Snail Mount' (G), which, although it is not clear from this picture how it did so, was supposed at one point to represent the Armada, in the guise of a monster with horns of wild-fire. Upon the lake floated a pinnace, a gift from 'gold-breasted India' to the Queen, which, with a nymph and her maidens in it singing, was drawn across the lake by Neptune and his attendants 'with grisly heads and beards of divers colours and fashions', to where Elizabeth sat enthroned at the water's edge at the western shore of the pond. Commentators have seen in this famous occasion some possibility that Shakespeare may have had it in mind when he was writing Oberon's speech in *A Midsummer Night's Dream*, about the 'fair Vestal throned by the West'.

From Nichol's Progresses of Queen Elizabeth

Plate 37 FESTIVAL CAR AND COSTUMES, BRUNSWICK, 1616

Photo: Oskar Fischel Collection

Plate 38 A WATER PAGEANT AT FLORENCE. Engraving by J. Callot

The principal feature is a ship blazing with fireworks. Note the ornate pageant cars in the foreground.

Photo: Oskar Fischel Collection

Plate 39 STAGING AT COURT, 1581

The method of the dispersed or simultaneous setting commonly used for courtly entertainments, before it was superseded by the Italian invention of the integrated perspective setting, is here illustrated in the frontispiece to the published (1582) account of Baltazarini's *Ballet Joyeux de la Reine*.

The settings are: In the background a triple arbour, with the Garden

of Circe before it, full of beasts. Seen through the arbour is Circe's palace, presumably painted on a cloth. Near the Garden stands an ornate
fountain. Forward on the left is a sort of Heaven, formed like an arcaded
enclosure made of star-spangled clouds, and facing it on the other side of
the floor is a Grove of Pan.

British Museum

SECTION IV. COSTUMES AND INDOOR THEATRES

Plate 40 A SCENE FROM 'TITUS ANDRONICUS'

This contemporary drawing is ascribed to the hand of Henry Peacham,
author of *The Complete Gentleman*, and is generally believed to date from
about 1594 or 1595, that is, it is more or less contemporary with the de
Witt sketch of the Swan theatre. In this connexion Professor J. Dover
Wilson has something to say [1] regarding the respective merits of the two
drawings. '. . . . I would point', he says, 'to the elaborate hypothetical
structures that have been erected from the material furnished by one
Dutchman's copy of another Dutchman's sketch of what he remembered
about the interior of the Swan theatre after a single visit, and ask whether
speculations based upon this [Titus Andronicus] much neglected, unique
and finished drawing of Shakespeare's fellows in action on his stage and
performing one of the plays of his canon, may not be more profitable.'

What concerns us here is the contemporary record of the costumes
worn. They comprise a mixture of contemporary dress (for the lesser characters) and an attempt at Roman dress for the principals. A comparison with
the costumes in the Tarquin play (Plate 26) shows an interesting similarity, especially in the case of Aaron's tunic, made in the style of Roman
armour, but (as can be clearly seen in the Tarquin pictures) of fabric or
leather. The treatment of Aaron as a coal-black blackamoor gives rise to
speculation about the usual way of representing moors on the Elizabethan stage, with of course its implication about Othello.

The use of scarves knotted on the shoulder should be noted.

Reproduced by permission of the Marquess of Bath, Longleat

Plate 41 COSTUMES IN THE ROMAN STYLE

These figures of Boadicea and Petillius Cerealis do not come from a
theatrical source, but are part of the ornament of a Jacobean map of

---

[1] *Shakespeare Survey I*, 1948.

Essex. It will be seen, however, that they are entirely in accord with the theatrical dresses shown in Plate 40. They are also similar to many of the theatrical designs of Inigo Jones (cf. Plate 59a).

This and the following plate are taken from John Speed's atlas *The Theatre of the Empire of Great Britain*. The engravings are by Jodocus Hondius, a Fleming, but the work was devised and published in England. The first edition appeared in 1611, but loose plates were in circulation at an earlier date, and the style of costume and decoration throughout the book may be accepted as a true reflection of the style which would have been considered correct in the theatre during Shakespeare's heyday.

British Museum

Plate 42 JOHN SPEED'S TITLE PAGE, 1614

It ought, perhaps, to be made clear that the word 'Theatre' in this title is strictly a coincidence: here it means only 'a scene of action' in a general sense, for the book is an atlas. However, it may be seen that the whole arrangement and detail of this delightful composition is in fact theatrical in character and corresponds entirely to what we have already seen of the style of the Flemish theatres and the English triumphal arches. Apart from this, there is a special interest in the figures shown here, for they are all labelled with the periods for which they are supposed to be historically representative, and there are in fact many attempts at historical accuracy, e.g., the top figure of a 'Britaine', moustachioed and woaded. At bottom right the 'Norman' is represented as wearing pointed medieval shoes—a deliberate historical archaism. But for the most part the historical element is fanciful and theatrical: the open robe of the 'Saxon', for instance, may be compared with the robes of the dramatic figures in Plate 43.

It is reasonable to suppose that this engraving would have been familiar to Shakespeare and his fellows, and it would be almost *un*reasonable to think that their own choice of costumes would not have been influenced by such pictures.

British Museum

Plate 43 BEN JONSON'S TITLE PAGE, 1616

It should first be noted that this engraving is from the hand not of a Flemish but of an English engraver, William Hole. It is also not improbable that Jonson himself may have had a hand in laying out the details of the design, especially in its classical allusions.

The figures represent Tragedy and Comedy, and (top) Tragi-Comedy, dressed in a half-and-half mixture of the style of the other two; the remaining large figures represent Satyrical and Pastoral drama. Above the title panel is a Jacobean (Jonson's?) idea of a Roman theatre, and at the foot of the page are two little panels representing what was then known of the Greek theatre: on the right an amphitheatre with a Chorus around the altar; on the left Thespis in his cart (but very much obscured!), to which is tethered the goat (*Tragos*) from which Tragedy derived its name.

British Museum

Plates 44 & 45 THE *MESSALINA* AND *ROXANA* TITLE PAGES

These two small engravings (here reproduced slightly larger than original size) are important as showing, each in the centre bottom panel, the only known pictures of *English* stages of Shakespearean or quasi-Shakespearean type, other than the Swan drawing and the 'Wits' frontispiece. Even so, they are a late reference, and their derivation is unsure. They are presumed by some authorities to represent college performances. Both show a background of hangings (the *Messalina* has tapestry) and a wedge-shaped stage with a railing. Except for the central upper opening of the *Messalina* stage, they could, and indeed they might, be the same place.

Of the two the *Roxana* is by far the better engraving. The 'classical' dramatic costumes are worth noting, as also the figure of Fame, which may be compared with that in Plate 25.

British Museum

Plate 46 THE MERMAID THEATRE, LONDON, 1951

This stage was designed for Mr. Bernard Miles by Michael Stringer and C. Walter Hodges. It was intended as a free experiment in the Elizabethan style, and not as a reconstruction in the antiquarian sense. It was used with success for productions not only of Elizabethan drama, but of Restoration opera. It is included here in order that something of the effect of the ornate style can be seen in living terms, as compared with the engravings on other pages.

Photo: Angus McBean

Plates 47, 48, 49 THE SCHOUWBURG, AMSTERDAM, 1658. Engraving by S. Savry
Before the "scenery theatre", with its proscenium frame, had established
itself as the pattern for all future theatre building in Europe, there were
one or two attempts made in the mid-seventeenth century to establish a
development of the old and traditional actors' stage in a permanent indoor setting. One such theatre was Shakespeare's Blackfriars (1608–55),
of which no stage details are known. Another was Jacob van Campen's
theatre in Amsterdam, the subject of these three engravings. This appears to have been a complete hybrid, having not only some of the quali-
ties of dispersed setting in the medieval style, with a King's throne in the
centre and a Heavens gallery above it, but also a rudimentary provision
for painted wings, which could be changeable, set between the pillars at
the sides. There is also a curtain provided, which can be hung across the
stage, leaving only a narrow apron in front of it, but this would seem to
have been awkwardly managed, if the arrangement shown in Plate 49
was the usual one. In accordance with a practice commonly found at
this period, the curtain was a striped one.

The wide, shallow layout of the auditorium is more related to the proportion of the Elizabethan theatre yard than to the horseshoe layout of
proscenium theatres. The Elizabethan touch and the derivation from the
popular street theatre is given also by the fact that the floor space was for
standing spectators, and that the stage, as can be judged by comparing
the level of the lower boxes with the figure coming in at the door in
Plate 47, was high.

Richard Southern Collection

Plate 50 DESIGN FOR THE COCKPIT-IN-COURT THEATRE, *c.* 1632
Formerly attributed to Inigo Jones, this design has been shown by William Grant Keith (*Architectural Review*, February 1925) to be not by Jones
but by his nephew and disciple John Webb. Whether the design was
ever in fact used, or whether it was only a project is also a question. However, like the Amsterdam Schouwburg, it is a good example of theatre
architecture at the period of indecision before the proscenium theatre
became the established form. In this particular case the old link with the
round or polygonal Bankside theatres is obvious. Here, too, is the influence of the thrust-out Elizabethan stage which was continued in the
large apron-stage of the Restoration and eighteenth-century London
theatres.

The attempt in this Cockpit design was to establish an architectural stage façade on classical lines, probably inspired by Palladio's famous Teatro Olimpico at Vicenza. It is, however, a curious feature of this design that, except for the big central archway, the entrances are only 5 feet high. The stage is 4½ feet back, 35 feet wide and 16 feet deep.

Worcester College Library, Oxford

SECTION V. TRICKS AND MACHINES

Plate 51 FURTENBACH'S THEATRICAL EFFECTS, 1663

Joseph Furtenbach, the author of *Mannhafter Kunst-Spiegel*, a work on scenic technique from which these engravings are taken, was born in 1591, and travelled in Italy between 1612 and 1622. Thus his book, which was published in Augsburg when Furtenbach was seventy-two, fairly represents the stage fashions of the first half of the seventeenth century. Although he is primarily concerned with proscenium-stage effects, many of the devices shown on this page are of a traditional character. If there had been illustrations to Philip Henslowe's property list given on p. 73, they would not have looked very different from this. The items are as follows (I shall refer to each row by the letter in the margin, and each picture by its number in the row, from left to right):

Row. A. Celestial effects. A1 is described by Furtenbach as 'a box 5 feet square and 4½ feet deep, with a back seat and two side seats for three angels, little boys dressed in white with red sashes and curly wigs. The inside of the box is covered with brass or gilt in a rough manner, so as to catch and reflect the light. Candles put inside, but carefully shaded. The outside is painted with angels' heads. The whole is lowered by a windlass arrangement and appears between other clouds.' No. A4 in the row shows a gilded box with an opening at back which is covered with a shutter, as shown in A3. The shutter is painted with clouds, but behind it is placed a glass of water with a light at the back, which shines out when the shutter is opened. Other shaded lights are placed at pp and oo in A4. A2 shows the complete arrangement. The sun in this, says Furtenbach, 'is made of brass . . . and polished with brick dust. The eye in the middle O is cut out, and an uneven glass flask filled with coloured water fixed into the hole, through which the light will shine in broken colours.

By an arrangement of rods this eye can be turned, and can thus shine and twinkle more. When God or Moses speaks, the whole sun is turned round.'

Row B. B1 is a counterweighted crane for lowering a painted cloud from the Heavens. An angel seated in the middle 'steps out when the cloud is lowered, fulfils his office, and is taken up again by the cloud'. B2 is a variation of B1. The angel sits between the painted clouds at the point marked RR. B3 is a device in a Jonah play: the prophet watches the fruit grow and decay before his eyes. The fruit is painted green on one side and rotting on the other, and the effect is gained simply by having it mechanically turned round. B4 is a throne for Pharaoh.

Row C. C1 shows three kinds of waves for sea effects. The top one is a cut-out ground row to stand against a backcloth. The middle one represents 'moving sea-waves; these are painted in a more lively style, pushed backwards and forwards on a rail'. At the bottom are 'very great waves; they have to be painted on fin-like protrusions and fixed with nails into a big wooden pole, which can be turned on the pivots yy like a spit'. C2 are also waves, but they are used 'for the passage of the Israelites through the Red Sea, and are put right and left into the floor, with a counterweight and rods attached to them at b, so that they can be lowered gradually in order to drown Pharaoh . . .' C3 is a painted rock, apparently with a pedestal at the top; perhaps intended for Moses on Mount Sinai.

Row D. D1: Jonah's Whale. 'It has globes and lights in its eyes, a hole on the far side by which Jonah can escape below the scene and rest until it is time for him to creep back into the fish and be spat out again. The whale can be raised and lowered on a hinge. . . . Its jaw is opened by a wire or string from above, and is weighted so that it closes over Jonah of its own accord when the wire is slackened.' D2: a boat to be moved along behind the waves (C1). It is pulled by cords at yy, and can be made to rock on a pivot. D3 is a device for the Burning Bush in the Moses play referred to above (C2 and C3). The parasol framework, decorated like a bush painted in gold, is hidden among naturally painted bushes. At the proper moment it is opened from below by invisible means, and, with lamps shining upon it, appears to burn.

Oskar Fischel Collection

Plate 52 A FANTASTIC ELEPHANT, by Inigo Jones
> *By permission of the Trustees of the Chatsworth Settlement*

Plate 53 THE NORWICH DRAGON

Snap the Dragon was a traditional feature of municipal pageantry in Norwich until the Reform of the Municipal Corporations in 1835. There are three versions of Snap at the Castle Museum, Norwich, all varying a little in detail. The one shown in this illustration is the oldest, and belongs to the eighteenth century. The idea, however, is considered to date back to the Middle Ages, and therefore may fairly be offered as an example of a popular theatrical device familiar in Elizabethan times. The effigy was carried on a harness over the shoulders of a man whose head poked out of the hole seen in the middle of the back, and whose legs were hidden by the skirt below. The carved wooden head is attached to a short pole which enabled the carrier to move it backwards and forwards and also to a limited extent from side to side. The jaws were raised and lowered by means of a string. The carved wooden wings are fixed. The body is coloured green, and the scales are outlined in gold.

> *Photo: A. E. Coe & Sons, Norwich*

Plate 54 MECHANICAL DEVILS, FIFTEENTH CENTURY

Among the scenes in Marlowe's *Doctor Faustus* which have been interpolated (probably by another hand) from the stock-in-trade of the medieval theatre there is one in which Faustus bids Mephistophilis fetch him a wife. Mephistophilis is reluctant, but then agrees, as follows:

> *Meph.* Well, wilt thou have one? Sit there till I come. I'll fetch thee a wife in the devil's name.   [*Exit.*
> *Re-enter* Mephistophilis *with a* Devil *drest like a Woman, with fireworks.*
> *Meph.* Tell me, Faustus, how dost thou like thy wife?
> *Faust.* A plague on her for a hot whore!

The long tradition behind this joke is well illustrated by the first of the four drawings here reproduced, from an Italian MS. belonging to the first half of the fifteenth century. It shows a mechanical figure of a woman mounted on an armature (shown in detail on her right) who at an appropriate moment turns into a devil. Her bat's wings are at first hanging down at her side, so that they resemble the long sleeves of a fashionable dress; her horns are concealed behind her head-dress. But at the pull of a string the wings and horns swivel round on a pivot and stand upright. At the same time the fireworks start blazing from her mouth and ears.

The second picture on this page shows a moving effigy of a great Devil, made up of articulated parts, some of which are shown in the sketches below. The Devil is enthroned upon a furnace.

Bavarian State Library, Munich

Plate 55 THEATRICAL FLYING APPARATUS, SEVENTEENTH CENTURY

This drawing shows a system of winding-drums, counterweights and escapements for a flying throne, and for the free flight of a Mercury and Cupids. The hoisting gear can be moved to any position along the joists which support them. The three frames marked RRR may represent traps from which the cupids can fly up from under the stage, or perhaps screens from behind which the lines can be attached to the flyers un-noticed, when required.

The drawing is one of a series which Edward Carrick (*Architectural Review*, August 1931) attributes to the Mauro brothers, and which may have been copied from the work of the famous Giacomo Torelli at a theatre in Venice between 1640 and 1645. However, the apparatus shown here is applicable to the ordinary Elizabethan theatre. Cranford Adams considers that the technique of free flying was first introduced on the London stage with Ariel in *The Tempest*. The flying throne, on the other hand, is a device which dates back at least as far as 1587, when Greene specifies the use of one in his *Alphonsus*.

Palatine Library, Parma

Plate 56 A JACOBEAN 'HEAVENS'

This ceiling is preserved in its original paint at Cullen House, Banff-shire, and is believed to date from the first decade of the seventeenth century. Its relevance to the present subject is discussed in Chapter 5, p. 70.

Photo: Country Life

SECTION VI. MASQUES

Plate 57 SIR HENRY UNTON'S WEDDING MASQUE

In its original form a masque represented the ceremonial visit with which some heroic or divine personage blessed a festive occasion. At an appro-priate moment of the evening the Visitor would enter from the world outside, accompanied by his torchbearers and musicians and by his knights, who would then take out the ladies of their choice from among the company, into the dance. This form still underlay all masquing in Shakespeare's time, though the addition of antimasques, and of dialogue and songs specially composed by poets, was gradually changing it into a more dramatic, though still very gracious form. Enormous sums of money were frequently spent on these entertainments.

The portrait of Sir Henry Unton (1557–96), which was finished after his death, shows him seated in the midst of a progression of scenes representing the principal events of his life, with his death and burial. Prominent among these scenes is his wedding feast and masque, the portion here reproduced. Sir Henry is shown seated in the centre of the table, bareheaded. His wife is at the end on the right. The masquers have entered, led and presented by a green-clad huntsman who is seen addressing Lady Unton. The torchbearers are naked children, in pairs, black and white, perhaps representing the Cupids of Night and Day. The principal masquers are Mercury, with Diana and her huntresses in pairs, each carrying either a garland or a bow and arrows. The masquers are dressed in a silver-coloured stuff patterned over with sprays of green leaves, with red flowers. Their head-dresses are of silver, garlanded, and their faces are covered with masks of red. The long scarves which the children wear trailing from their heads are parti-coloured in red and white. At the right, half-hidden by the pillar, is a taborer. The procession is reminiscent of the nuptial procession of the fairies through the house of Theseus at the end of *A Midsummer Night's Dream*.

National Portrait Gallery, London

Plates 58 & 59 INIGO JONES. DESIGNS FOR THE MASQUE OF 'OBERON', 1611

Inigo Jones (1573–1651), after studying painting and architecture in Italy, returned to England in 1605, where he was at once employed as architect and designer to Anne, James I's Queen. His designs for Court Masques were based upon the Italian style, and were of such inventive magnificence as eventually to incur the wrath of his collaborator, Ben Jonson, who held that this 'painting and carpentry' should not be allowed to usurp the admiration which more properly belonged to poetry, for which it was supposed to be only an adornment. That, however, refers particularly to the more elaborate masques of Charles I's reign. The designs reproduced

here have all been chosen from those made in Jones's earliest period, during the lifetime of Shakespeare. The *Oberon* series are the first extant
examples in the history of the English theatre of scenery and costumes
designed by the same artist.

Oberon, the Faery Prince, was presented in the Banqueting House,
Whitehall, on January 1st, 1611, by Henry Frederick, Prince of Wales,
who himself appeared as Oberon. The first scene showed a rocky cliff,
in front of which the antimasque was performed by Satyrs. The cliff
then opened and revealed the front of 'a bright and glorious *Palace*, whose
gates and walls were transparent'. After some dancing, and at the crow-
ing of a cock, this in its turn opened and revealed 'the nation of Faies',
with Oberon in a chariot drawn by two white bears, and the knightly
masquers ranked on seats around him. The principal dances of the
masque then took place.

Plate 58 shows two of the scenes for this. At the bottom (right) is the
rocky cliff for the antimasque. Above is the front of Oberon's palace.
Below, left, is a detail sketch for part of this, upon the back of which
Inigo Jones has noted down the dimensions: the 'heyght of the middell
space' was 9 feet, and its breadth 5 feet; the height of the towers at the
side, to the level of their battlements, was 11 feet; of the columns on the
first storey, 7 feet; and of the 'terms', i.e., the caryatid-like figures carrying the pediment, 4 feet 1 inch. In both drawings the spaces for the transparency mentioned above can be seen.

There are two other drawings in the Chatsworth collection which are
related to the Oberon's Palace scene and which have been published
under that title. Judging partly from the style in which these latter are
drawn, however (they are in a freer style of drawing, more typical of
Jones's later work), Richard Southern has suggested to me that although
they were based upon the original Oberon designs (published here) they
are probably adaptations for another occasion at a later date. Plate 59
gives some of the costumes for *Oberon*. At top, left, is a Knight Masquer.
The others are all 'Faies'.

By permission of the Trustees of the Chatsworth Settlement

Plate 60 INIGO JONES: DRESS DESIGN FOR AN OCEANID AS TORCHBEARER. From
the *Masque of Blackness*, 1605

By permission of the Trustees of the Chatsworth Settlement

Plate 61   INIGO JONES: DRESS DESIGN FOR IRIS. From the Masque *Hymenaei*,
      1606
         From the Devonshire Collection, Chatsworth.   *Reproduced by permission*
         of the Trustees of the Chatsworth Settlement

Plate 62   A LADY IN MASQUE COSTUME, *c.* 1610.   Enlarged from a miniature by
      Isaac Oliver
         Crown Copyright reserved. Victoria and Albert Museum, London

From *The Fables of Phædrus*, Amsterdam, 1688

1. LONDON FROM BANKSIDE, SHOWING THE GLOBE AND THE BEAR-GARDEN

From the engraving by J. C. Visscher, *c.* 1616

2. BANKSIDE, SHOWING THE PLAYHOUSES, 1600

From John Norden's revised version of his earlier (1593) map of London

St. Mary Overies
(Southwark Cathedral)

Bear-garden   Rose
Globe

Swan

London
Bridge

Cannon Street
Station

Southwark Bridge

Southwark Cathedral

Bear-garden
Rose
Globe

300 feet

3. AIR VIEW OF BANKSIDE, 1949

Convent garden   S. Clement

Somerset E.   Arundel house   Essex house   Temple stayres   Temple   Blackfreyars

The Globe

Bay

Beere bayting

4. BANKSIDE SHOWING THE THEATRES (WIT

From the

S.Pauwls Church

S. ye Waterhouse

S. Andre in Holborne

Paulus wharfe

Queene hythe

The 3. Cranes

the Eel Ships

Winchester house

ES REVERSED) SHORTLY BEFORE 1644

el Hollar

5. ORIGINAL DRAWING OF THE SECOND GLOBE AND THE BEAR-GARDEN
By Wenzel Hollar

Swan   Bear-garden   Rose   Globe

6. BANKSIDE
Detail from the *Civitas Londini* view, 1600

tectum

porticus

sedilia

orchestra

ingressus

mimorum
ædes

proscænium

planties sive arena

quintum sed vispari et structura, bestiarum concretati
oni destinatum, in quo multi ursi, tauri, et stupenda
magnitudinis canes, distinctis caueis & septis aluntur, qui
ad

7. THE SWAN THEATRE, *c.* 1596

The Globe on Bank Side Where Shakespere Acted

8 and 9. DEBASED EIGHTEENTH-CENTURY VERSIONS OF THE GLOBE

Plain near SHREWSBURY

10. THE GLOBE: AN EARLY ATTEMPT AT RECONSTRUCTION

11. THE GLOBE: A RECONSTRUCTION OF 1910

K

12. AN OPENING FROM HENSLOWE'S DIARY FOR 1597–98

13. PORTION OF A LETTER FROM EDWARD ALLEYN TO
HIS WIFE

14. 'THE PLATT OF THE SECOND PART OF THE SEVEN DEADLY SINS'

15. THE STAGE FOR 'LAURENTIUS', COLOGNE, 1581

16. A FLEMISH STREET THEATRE, c. 1650

17. A MOUNTEBANK STAGE, *c.* 1600

18. A STREET THEATRE IN LOUVAIN, 1594

19. CHRIST SHOWN TO THE PEOPLE

Etching (1st state) by Rembrandt, 1655

20. STAGE IN BRUSSELS, 1594

21. FLEMISH STREET THEATRE, 1607

22. BASQUE FOLK-DANCE STAGE, *c.* 1934

Within the illustration: SCARRONS COMICAL ROMANCE OF: A Company of Stage Players.

23. ENGLISH STREET THEATRE AND PLAYERS, 1676

L

24. DETAIL FROM 'THE TRIUMPH OF ISABELLA', 1615 (THE CAR OF THE NATIVITY)

25. DETAIL FROM 'THE TRIUMPH OF ISABELLA', 1615 (THE CAR OF ISABELLA AND HER COURT)

140

ALDVS WAS HET TOONNEEL, ST.

26. THE TARQU

28. STREET THEATRE, GHENT, 1539

27. REDERYKER STAGE, ANTWERP, 1582

30. THE TRIUMPH OF JAMES I, LONDON,
1604: (2) THE TEMPLE OF JANUS

29. THE TRIUMPH OF JAMES I, LONDON,
1604: (1) THE FLEMISH ARCH

31. THE TRIUMPH OF JAMES I, LONDON, 1604: (3) THE ARCH OF LONDON

S. H. Excud:

32. THE TRIUMPH OF JAMES I, LONDON, 1604: (4) THE GARDEN OF PLENTY

M

33. THE TRIUMPH OF JAMES I, LONDON, 1604: (5) THE NEW ARABIA FELIX

34. THE TRIUMPH OF JAMES I, LONDON, 1604: (6) THE ARCH OF THE NEW
WORLD

35. THE CHARIOT OF ROYAL JUSTICE

36. THE ELVETHAM ENTERTAINMENT FOR QUEEN ELIZABETH I, 1591

37. FESTIVAL CAR AND COSTUMES, BRUNSWICK, 1616

38. A WATER PAGEANT AT FLORENCE
Engraving by J. Callot

39. STAGING AT COURT, 1581

40. A SCENE FROM 'TITUS ANDRONICUS', *c.* 1595

41. COSTUMES IN THE ROMAN STYLE, *c.* 1611

A BRITAINE

A ROMANE

A SAXON

BRITANNIA

A DANE

A NORMAN

THE
THEATRE
OF THE EMPIRE
OF GREAT
BRITAINE:
Presenting
AN EXACT GEOGRAPHY
of the Kingdomes of ENGLAND,
SCOTLAND, IRELAND,
and the ILES adioyning:
with
The Shires, Hundreds, Cities and
Shire-townes, within ý Kingdome
of ENGLAND, divided and
described
By
IOHN SPEED.

IMPRINTED AT LONDON

Anno
Cum Privilegio
1614

And are to be solde by Iohn Sudbury & Georg
Humble, in Popes head alley at ý signe of ý white Horse.

42. JOHN SPEED'S TITLE PAGE, 1614

43. BEN JONSON'S TITLE PAGE, 1616

154

45. THE 'ROXANA' TITLE PAGE, 1632

44. THE 'MESSALINA' TITLE PAGE, 1640

46. THE MERMAID THEATRE, LONDON, 1951

47. THE SCHOUWBURG, AMSTERDAM, 1658: THE AUDITORIUM

48. THE SCHOUWBURG, AMSTERDAM, 1658: GROUND PLAN

DE SCHOUBURGH van binnen
op 't Tooneel aen te sien

49. THE SCHOUWBURG, AMSTERDAM, 1658: THE STAGE

50. DESIGN FOR THE COCKPIT-IN-COURT THEATRE, LONDON, *c.* 1632

51. FURTENBACH'S THEATRICAL EFFECTS, 1663

52. A FANTASTIC ELEPHANT, BY INIGO JONES

53. THE NORWICH DRAGON

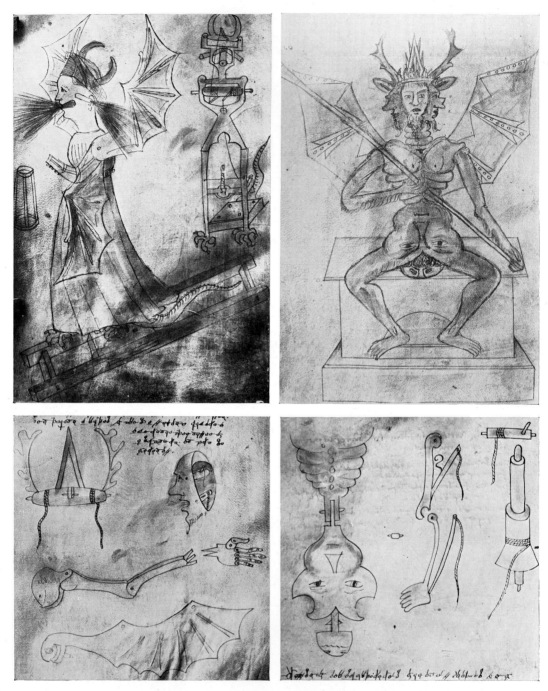

54. MECHANICAL DEVILS, FIFTEENTH CENTURY

55. THEATRICAL FLYING APPARATUS, SEVENTEENTH CENTURY

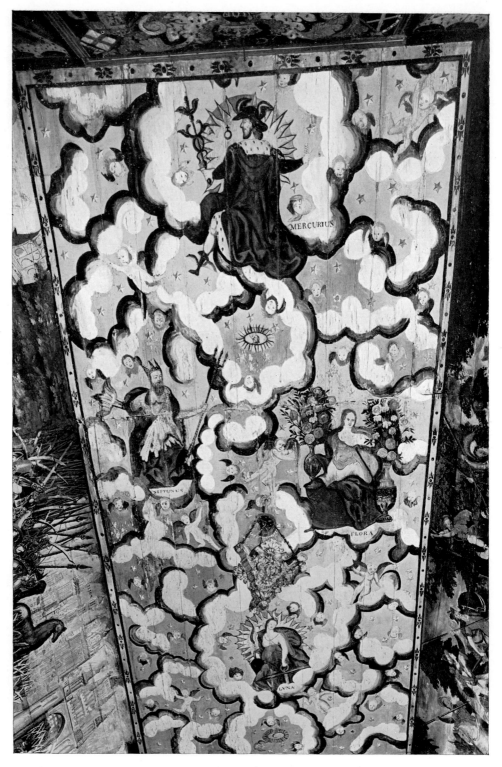

56. A JACOBEAN 'HEAVENS' AT CULLEN, BANFFSHIRE

57. SIR HENRY UNTON'S WEDDING MASQUE, *c.* 1597

58. INIGO JONES. SCENERY FOR THE MASQUE OF 'OBERON', 1611

59. INIGO JONES. COSTUMES FOR THE MASQUE OF 'OBERON', 1611

60. INIGO JONES.   AN OCEANID AS TORCHBEARER

Dress Design from the *Masque of Blackness*, 1605

61. INIGO JONES. IRIS

Dress Design from the Masque *Hymenaei*, 1606

62. A LADY IN MASQUE COSTUME, *c.* 1610

Enlarged from a miniature by Isaac Oliver

Appendixes

APPENDIX A

RECONSTRUCTIONS

1. Stage in an Inn-Yard, *c.* 1565

The stage shown here is based upon two pictures, one from the sixteenth century by Pieter Balten, and the other from the seventeenth by Callot (reproduced on p. ix of this book). The stages they show are almost identical. The sketch above is intended to represent a provincial fit-up. In the more firmly established conditions obtaining for a while at the great London inns this arrangement may have been modified somewhat, the stage perhaps being married up with the surrounding buildings, but the general effect was probably much the same.

2. Stage in an Amphitheatre, *c.* 1576

The little stage and booth has now been moved into an arena, but it can be dismounted and removed if the yard is wanted for the 'game of bulls and bears'. When the stage is in position the galleries adjoining it are taken over as back-stage area. The top of the booth has here been boarded over and railed in, so that it can be used as an acting place, and it is rather more elaborately decorated than formerly.

3. Development 1580–90 (i)

This sketch and the following one represent possible intermediate steps in the early development of the theatres. The one above shows the direct line of development from the previous one (sketch 2). It is supposed that the stage has now become permanent. It has been enlarged, and stands no longer upon trestles but upon posts with curtains hung between. A stage trap can be seen. The booth, however, has here not enlarged itself, but remains as an individual enclosure within the structure that has grown up around it.

Musicians

Lords'
Room
(and/or
upper Stage)

Tiring
House

Stairs
to
Gallery

Entrance

Entrance

4. Development 1580–90 (ii)

This shows an alternative development. In this case it is assumed that the booth as well as the stage has been enlarged, built up and ornamented in the Baroque style, as in the Flemish theatres. It may have been at this point that it became necessary to consider having a roof over the stage, partly to shelter the actors and stage furniture from the weather, partly perhaps to keep the afternoon sun out of the eyes of the audience, but chiefly to provide the spectacle of heavenly apparitions descending from above.

5. A Playhouse, c. 1595

This sketch is based upon the Swan drawing. The top-storey opening within the Heavens is conjectural. The position of the Heavens is conjectural. The position of the Heavens hut, set fairly low within the encircling roof, is in accordance with several authentic views (cf. Plates 2 and 6). The main weight of the hut is here carried upon the line of the tiring-house façade.

6. The Fortune Theatre, 1600

The overall dimensions and layout are according to the contract, but details are necessarily conjectural. I here assume that the building was set with the tiring-house backing on to the street, and that the audience entered the yard along the gangways on either side of the stage. 'Iron pikes', as in the contract, are placed along the parapet of the bottom gallery to prevent persons climbing over from the yard. Upper galleries are reached by stairs in the angles of the building near the street.

7. The Hope Theatre, 1614

The discovery of the reversal of the names of the theatres in Hollar's view of Bankside (Plate 4) now enables us to reconstruct the conditions given in the Hope contract. The curious peak in the roof shown in the Hollar print indicates the way the builder solved his problem of constructing the Heavens 'without any posts or supporters' upon the stage. By raising the ridge-line on that side it was possible to give the inward-sloping members of the roof a long reach into and over the middle of the yard, thus supporting the Heavens from above as if by a sort of crane. Additional strength would be given to this by the fact of building on an interior curve. Since, however, the long lines of the roof overhanging the yard would have had a rather oppressive appearance, I suggest that this might have been minimised by erecting an ornamental fascia.

8. The Second Globe, 1614

Following the Hollar print, I here show a greatly enlarged Heavens which, for stability, is now joined to the sides of the main building. This entails raising the ceiling to the height of the eaves, so as to avoid loss of light. I have also assumed that it may have been at this stage of theatre development that the traditional flat façade of the tiring-house began to give way to new influences, and I show a curved façade somewhat resembling the Cockpit drawing in Plate 50.

APPENDIX B

THE LONDON THEATRES 1576–1660

Theatre.	Principal Occupying Companies.	Managements.	Built.	Demolished.	Remarks.
Public Theatres					
The Theatre	The Chamberlain's (Lord Hunsdon's) Men.	James Burbage and associates.	1576	1598	The Queen's Men, with Richard Tarlton, sometimes acted here in the 1580s.
The Curtain	The Chamberlain's (Lord Hunsdon's) Men.	Henry Lanman. Sometimes in association with James Burbage.	1577–8	Not heard of after 1627.[1]	After 1603 this theatre became associated with Worcester's (later Queen's) Men.
Newington Butts	The Lord Admiral's Men and others.	Philip Henslowe.	? 1579	? 1599	—
The Rose	The Lord Admiral's Men.	Philip Henslowe.	1587	Nothing directly known after 1605.	But tithes still due from the property in 1622.
The Swan	—	Francis Langley.	c. 1594	c. 1614	Henslowe may have had an interest in it after Langley's death in 1601.
The Fortune	The Lord Admiral's Men.	Philip Henslowe and Edward Alleyn.	1600	Dismantled 1649.	Destroyed by fire in 1621, but rebuilt 1623. Finally demolished 1662.
The Globe I	The Chamberlain's (later King's) Men.	Cuthbert and Richard Burbage and associates (incl. Wm. Shakespeare).	1599	1613	Built with the timbers of the old Theatre. Destroyed by fire.
The Globe II	The King's Men.	„	1614	1644	—

Theatre	Company	Proprietors / Masters	Built	Last heard of in the 1660s.	Altered or enlarged (roofed?) c. 1625.
The Red Bull	The Earl of Worcester's (The Queen's) Men.	Aaron Holland and others.	? 1606		Altered or enlarged (roofed?) c. 1625.
The Hope	Lady Elizabeth's Men until 1615.	Philip Henslowe, Edward Alleyn, Jacob Meade.	1613–14	1656	Built over the site of the original Bear-garden.
Private Theatres					
Blackfriars I	Children of the Chapel (Queen's Revels).	Masters: William Hunnis. Richard Farrant Henry Evans.	1576	Converted 1584.	James Burbage leases and converts hall to theatre for own use in 1596, but does not then occupy. Leases to Evans and Giles in 1600, until 1608.
Blackfriars II *(a)*	,,	Henry Evans, Nathaniel Giles.	1600	1608	
Blackfriars II *(b)*	The King's Men.	Cuthbert and Richard Burbage and associates.	1608	1655	—
St. Paul's	The Children of Paul's.	Masters: Sebastian Westcott, d. 1582. 1586 Thomas Giles. 1599 Edward Peers.	c. 1557	c. 1608	Acted at Court and sometimes at Blackfriars. Location of own house not known; it may have been the St. Paul's singing school, or else the Convocation House.
Whitefriars	Children of the King's Revels. (Composed from former children's companies?)	—	c. 1606	1629	After 1609 Whitefriars occupied by different companies with indifferent success. After 1629 replaced by Salisbury Court. Replaced in Restoration times by Dorset Garden.
Salisbury Court	Queen Henrietta's Men: Prince's Men.	—	1629	1649	
The Cockpit, Drury Lane	The Earl of Worcester's (Queen Anne's) Men.	Christopher Beeston.	1616	—	Continues into Restoration times.

¹ Leslie Hotson (*Commonwealth and Restoration Stage*, p. 92) quotes a reference which seems to show that this theatre was still standing in 1660.

A Juste a count of all suche money as J haue layd owt for my lord admeralles players begyning the xj of octobr whose names ar as foloweth borne gabrell shaw Jonnes dowten Jube towne synger & the ij geffes 1597

layd owt unto Robarte shawe to by a boocke for the companey the 21 of octobr 1597 the some of called the cobler   wittnes E Alleyn } xxxx^s

lent unto Robarte shaw to by a boocke of yonge harton the 5 of novembr 1597 the some of... wittnes E Alleyn } x^s

lent unto Robart shaw for the companey to bye viij yrdes of clothe of gow[e]lde for the womanes gowne in bran howlte the 26 of novembr 1597 the some of .... } iiij^{ll}

lent unto Robart shawe to geue the tayller to by tynsell for bornes gowne the j of desembr 1597 ix^s

layd owt for the companye to by tafetie & tynssell for the bodeyes of a womanes gowne to play allce perce wch j dd unto the littel tayller the 8 desembr 1597 .... } xx^s
wittnes E Alleyn

layd owt for mackynge allce perces bodeyes & a payer of yeare sleaues the some of.............. vj^s vij^d

lent unto Bengeman Johnson[1] the 3 of desembr 1597 upon a booke wch he showed the plotte vnto the company wch he promysed to dd vnto the company at cryssmas next the some of ... } xx^s

lent unto Robart shawe to by copr lace of sylver for a payer of hosse in allce perce the 10 of desembr 1597 .... } xvj^s
witness wm borne Jube & gabrell spenser[2]

layd owt for ij gyges for the companey to ij yonge men the 12 of desembr 1597 the some of vj^s 8^d

layd owt the 22 of desembr 1597 for a boocke called mother Read cape to antony monday & drayton .... } iij^{ll}

layd owt the 28 of desembr 1597 for a boocke called mother Read cape to antoney mondaye v^s

lent the company to bye a flame coler satten dublett the 5 of Janeway 1597 the some of ...... xxxxv^s

---

[1] At this date Ben Jonson was known only as an actor and (with Nashe) part-author of *The Isle of Dogs*, a satirical play, now lost, which had caused great official displeasure. Indeed, it was only just two months before this entry of Henslowe's that Jonson was released from the Marshalsea prison, where he had been committed for his complicity in the play, both as actor and author. His first great success, *Every Man in His Humour*, did not come on to the stage till the September of the year following this entry, and then was put on by the Chamberlain's Men, Henslowe's competitors. The book referred to in this entry is not known, and it seems Jonson failed to deliver it.

[2] Gabriel Spenser's name appearing in this entry, following so close upon the reference to Ben Jonson, is interesting.   At this time Spenser was one of Henslowe's

HENSLOWE'S DIARY (See Plate 12)

layd owt for my ord admeralles meane as foloweth 1597
1597

---

pd unto antony monday & drayton for the laste payment of the Boocke of mother Readcape} lv^s
the 5 of Janewary 1597 the some of ....

for the littel boye
Layd owte for copr lace ∧ & for a valle for the boye a geanste the playe of dido & eneus the 3 of} xxix^s
Jeneway 1597 ....

Lent vnto thomas dowton the 8 of Janewary 1597 twenty shillinges to by a boockes of mr} xx^s
dickers³ lent...

Lent vnto the company when they fyrst played dido at nyght the some of thirtishillynges wch} xxx^s
warse the 8 of Jeneway 1597 J saye ....

lent vnto the company the 15 of Jeneway 1597⁴ to bye a boocke of mr dicker called fayeton} iiij^ll
fower pownde J saye lent ....

lent vnto Thomas dowton for the company to bye a sewte for phayeton & ij Rebates & j} iij^ll
fardengalle the 26 of Jeneway 1598 the some of three pownde J saye lent ....

lent vnto Thomas dowton the 28 of Jeneway 1598 to bye a whitte satten dublett for phayeton} xxxx^s
fortyshyllenges J saye lent ....

lent vnto the companey the 4 of febreary 1598 to dise charge my dicker owt of the cownter in} xxxx^s
the powltrey⁵ the some of fortie shillinges J saye dd to thomas dowton...........................

Layd owt vnto antony monday the 15 of febreary 1598 for a playe boocke called the firste parte} v^ll
of Robyne hoode ....

---

best actors. Earlier he had shared imprisonment with
Jonson over the *Isle of Dogs* affair (cf. footnote 1 above).
But nine months after this diary entry (and incidentally
just two days after the first production of Jonson's *Every
Man in His Humour*) he and Jonson quarrelled violently,
and fought a duel in the fields at Shoreditch, near the
Theatre. Spenser was slain outright, and Jonson was
committed to prison once again. He was able to plead
benefit of clergy, and so was eventually released with the
forfeiture of his goods and with a branding on the
thumb—the letter T, the felon's mark of Tyburn. On

26th September 1598 Henslowe wrote in a letter to his
son-in-law, Edward Alleyn: 'Since you were with me
I have lost one of my company, which hurteth me
greatly, that is Gabriel, for he is slain in Hogsden Fields
by the hands of Benjamin Jonson. . . .'
³ *Mr. Dickers* = Thomas Dekker, the playwright.
⁴ Note that although the new year is already a fortnight
old, Henslowe is still writing 1597 instead of 1598!
⁵ *The Counter in the Poultry*. A prison where Dekker appears to have been detained for debt.

APPENDIX D

THE PLATT OF THE SECOUND PARTE OF THE
SEVEN DEADLIE SINNS

A tent being plast on the stage for Henry the Sixt. He in it asleepe. To him the Lieutenenant, a Purcevant, R. Cowley Jo Duke, & 1 Warder, R. Pallant. to them Pride, Gluttony, Wrath and Covetousnes at one dore. at another dore Envie, Sloth and Lechery. The three put back the foure and so exeunt.

Henry awaking Enter a Keeper J. Sincler. to him a Servaunt T. Belt to him Lidgate, & the Keeper Exit. then enter againe. Then Envy passeth over the stag. Lidgate speakes.

A Senitt. Dumb show.
Enter King Gorboduk wth Counsailers. R. Burbadg Mr Brian Th. Goodale. The Queene with Ferrex and Porrex and som attendaunts follow. Saunder. W. Sly. Harry. J. Duke, Kitt. R⁰ Pallant. J. Holland. After Gorboduk hath consulted with his lords he brings his 2 sonns to several seates. They *enving* on on other Ferrex offers to take Porex his Corowne. he draws his weapon. The King Queene and Lords step betweene them. They thrust them away and menasing ech other exit. The Queene and Lords depart hevilie. Lidgate speakes.

Enter Ferrex crownd with drum & coulers and soldiers one way. Harry. Kitt. R. Cowley John Duke. to them at another dore Porrex drum & collors & soldiers. W. Sly, R. Pallant. John Sincler, J. Holland.

Enter queene with 2 counsailors Mr. Brian Tho Goodale. to them Ferrex and Porrex several waies with drums and powers. Gorboduk entering in the midst between. Henry speakes.

Alarums with excurtions. After Lidgate speakes.

Enter Ferrex and Porrex severally Gorboduk still following them. Lucius Damasus Mr. Bry T. Good.

Enter Ferrex at one dore. Porrex at another. The fight. Ferrex is slayne. To them Videna the Queene. to her Damasus. to him Lucius.

Enter Porrex sad with Dordan his man. R.P.W. Sly. To them the Queene and a Ladie. Nich. Saunder. and Lords R. Cowly Mr. Brian. To them Lucius running.

Henry and Lidgat speaks. Sloth passeth over.

Enter Giraldus Phronesius Aspatia Pompeia Rodope. R. Cowly. Th. Goodale. R. Go. Ned. Nick.

Enter Sardinapalus Arbactus Nicanor and Captaines marching. Mr. Phillipps, Mr. Pope, R. Pa. Kit. J. Sincler. J. Holland.

Enter a Captaine with Aspatia and the Ladies. Kitt.

Lidgat speake.
Enter Nicanor wth other Captaines R. Pall. J. Sincler. Kitt. J. Holland. R. Cowly. to them Arbactus Mr. Pope. to him Will Foole J. Duke. to him Rodopeie Ned. to her Sardanapalus like a woman wth Aspatia Rodope Pompeia Will. Foole. to them Arbactus & 3 musitions Mr. Pope J. Sincler. Vincent. R. Cowly. to them Nicanor and others R. P. Kitt.

Enter Sardanapa. wth the Ladies. to them a Messenger Tho Goodale. to him Will Foole running. Alarum.

Enter Arbactus pursuing Sardanapalus. and the Ladies fly. After enter Sarda. with as many jewels robes and gold as he can cary.

Alarum.

Enter Arbactus Nicanor and the other Captains in triumph. Mr. Pope R. Pa. Kitt J. Holl. R. Cow. J. Sinc.

Henry speakes and Lidgate. Lechery passeth over the stag.

Enter Tereus Philomela Julio. R. Burbadge Ro. R. Pall. J. Sink.

Enter Progne Itis and Lords. Saunder. Will. J. Duke. W. Sly. Harry.

Enter Philomele and Tereus, to them Julio.

Enter Progne Panthea Itis amd Lords. Sander. T. Belt. Will. W. Sly. Hary. Th. Goodale. to them Tereus with Lords R. Burbadge. J. Duk. R. Cowley.

A dumb show. Lidgate speaks.

Enter Progne with the sampler. to her Tereus from hunting wth his Lords. to them Philomele with Itis hed in a dish. Mercury comes and all vanish. to him 3 Lords. Th. Goodale. Harey. W. Sly.

Henry speaks to him Lieutenant Pursevaunt and Warders. R. Cowley J. Duke J. Holland. Joh. Sincler. to them Warwick Mr. Brian.

Lidgate speaks to the audiens and so Exitts.

APPENDIX E

THE PLOT OF THE PLAY CALLED ENGLAND'S JOY

To be played at the Swan this 6 of November, 1602.

First, there is induct by show and in action, the civil wars of England from Edward the Third to the end of Queen Mary's reign, with the overthrow of usurpation.

2. Secondly then the entrance of England's Joy by the Coronation of our Sovereign Lady Elizabeth; her Throne attended with Peace, Plenty and Civil Policy: a sacred prelate standing at her right hand, betokening the serenity of the Gospel; at her left hand Justice; and at her feet War, with a scarlet robe of peace upon his armour; a wreath of bays about his temples, and a branch of palm in his hand.

3. Thirdly is dragged in three Furies, presenting Dissension, Famine, and Bloodshed, which are thrown into hell.

4. Fourthly is expressed under the person of a Tyrant, the envy of Spain, who to show his cruelty, causeth his soldiers drag in a beautiful Lady, whom they mangle and wound, tearing her garments and jewels from off her; and so leave her bloody, with her hair about her shoulders, lying upon the ground. To her come certain gentlemen, who seeing her piteous despoilment, turn to the Throne of England, from whence one descendeth, taketh up the Lady, wipeth her eyes, bindeth up her wounds, giveth her treasure, and bringeth forth a band of soldiers, who attend her forth. This Lady presenteth Belgia.

5. Fifthly, the Tyrant more enraged, taketh counsel, sends forth letters, privy spies and secret underminers, taking their oaths and giving them bags of treasure. These signify Lopus,[1] and certain Jesuits, who afterward, when the Tyrant looks for an answer from them, are showed to him in a glass with halters about their necks, which makes him mad with fury.

6. Sixthly, the Tyrant, seeing all secret means to fail him, intendeth upon violence and invasion by the hand of War, whereupon is set forth the battle at Sea in '88, with Englands victory.

7. Seventhly, he complotteth with the Irish rebels, wherein is laid open the base ingratitude of Tyrone, the landing there of Don John de Aguila, and their dissipation by the wisdom and valour of the Lord Mountjoy.

---

[1] *Lopus.* Doctor Ruy Lopez, an elderly physician popularly supposed to have been involved in a plot to poison the Queen. He was executed at Tyburn in 1594.

8. Eighthly, a great triumph is made with fighting of twelve gentlemen at Barriers, and sundry rewards sent from the Throne of England, to all sorts of well deservers.

9. Lastly, the Nine Worthies, with several coronets, present themselves before the Throne, which are put back by certain in the habit of Angels, who set upon the Lady's head which represents her Majesty, an Imperial Crown, garnished with the sun, moon and stars. And so with music both with voice and instruments she is taken up into Heaven, when presently appears a Throne of blessed souls, and beneath under the stage set forth with strange fireworks, divers black and damned souls, wonderfully described in their several torments.

[*Note:* The foregoing is the full text of a playbill, though whether or not there was ever a play to support it is open to question. The author of the bill, Richard Venner, claimed in after years that there had been, but that just before the play was due to begin he was intercepted by bailiffs who 'seizing me before the first entrance, spoke an Epilogue instead of a Prologue'. At all events, nothing went on to the stage, and the occasion itself became a byword. Even ten years later, in *Love Restored*, Jonson speaks of 'a fine trick, a piece of England's Joy'. What happened that day at the Swan is told in a letter written by John Chamberlain :

'. . . And, now we are in mirth, I must not forget to tell you of a cozening prank of one Venner, of Lincoln's Inn, that gave out bills of a famous play on Saturday was sevennight on the Bankside, to be acted only by certain gentlemen and gentlewomen of account. The price at coming in was two shillings or eighteen pence at least; and, when he had gotten most part of the money into his hands, he would have showed them a fair pair of heels, but he was not so nimble to get up on horseback, but that he was fain to forsake that course, and betake himself to the water, where he was pursued and taken, and brought before the Lord Chief Justice, who would make nothing of it but a jest and a merriment, and bound him over in five pound to appear at the sessions. In the mean time the common people, when they saw themselves deluded, revenged themselves upon the hangings, curtains, chairs, stools, walls and whatsoever came in their way, very outrageously, and made great spoil; there was great store of good company and many noblemen.']

APPENDIX F

THE CONTRACT FOR BUILDING
THE FORTUNE THEATRE, 1599

(From the text given by Dr. W. W. Greg in *Henslowe Papers*)

This Indenture made the Eighte daie of Januarye 1599, and in the Twoe and Fortyth
yeare of the Reigne of our sovereigne Ladie Elizabeth, by the grace of god Queene of
Englande, Fraunce and Irelande, defender of the Faythe, &c. betwene Phillipp Henslowe
and Edwarde Allen of the parishe of Ste Saviours in Southwark in the Countie of Surrey,
gentlemen, on thone parte, and Peeter Streete, Cittizen and Carpenter of London, on
thother parte witnesseth That whereas the saide Phillipp Henslowe & Edward Allen, the
daie of the date hereof, haue bargayned, compounded & agreed with the saide Peter
Streete ffor the erectinge, buildinge & settinge upp of a new howse and Stadge for a
Plaiehouse in and vppon a certeine plott or parcell of grounde appoynted oute for that
purpose, scytuate and beinge nere Goldinge lane in the parishe of Ste Giles withoute
Cripplegate of London, to be by him the saide Peeter Streete or somme other sufficyent
woorkmen of his provideinge and appoyntemente and att his propper costes & chardges,
for the consideracion hereafter in theis presentes expressed, made, erected, builded and
sett upp in manner & forme followinge (that is to saie); The frame of the saide howse to
be sett square and to conteine ffowerscore foote of lawfull assize everye waie square with-
outt and fiftie fiue foote of like assize square everye waie within, with a good suer and
stronge foundacion of pyles, brick, lyme and sand bothe without & within, to be
wroughte one foote of assize att the leiste aboue the grounde; And the saide fframe to
conteine three Stories in heighth, the first or lower Storie to conteine Twelue foote of
lawfull assize in heighth, the second Storie Eleauen foote of lawfull assize in heigth, and
the third or vpper Storie to conteine Nyne foote of lawfull assize in height; All which
Stories shall conteine Twelue foote and a halfe of lawfull assize in breadth througheoute,
besides a juttey forwardes in either of the saide twoe vpper Stories of Tenne ynches of
lawfull assize, with ffower convenient divisions for gentlemens roomes, and other
sufficient and convenient divisions for Twoe pennie roomes, with necessarie seates to be
placed and sett, aswell in those roomes as througheoute all the rest of the galleries of the
saide howse, and with suchelike steares, conveyances & divisions withoute & within, as
are made & contryved in and to the late erected Plaiehowse on the Banck in the saide
parishe of Ste Saviours called the Globe; With a Stadge and Tyreinge howse to be made,
erected & settupp within the saide fframe, with a shadowe or cover over the saide
Stadge, which Stadge shalbe placed & sett, as alsoe the stearecases of the saide fframe, in
suche sorte as is prefigured in a plott thereof drawen,[1] and which Stadge shall conteine in

[1] This " plott " does not now exist.

187

length Fortie and Three foote of lawfull assize and in breadth to extende to the middle of
the yarde of the saide howse; The same Stadge to be paled in belowe with good, stronge
and sufficyent newe oken bourdes, and likewise the lower Storie of the saide fframe
withinside, and the same lower storie to be alsoe laide over and fenced with strong yron
pykes; And the saide Stadge to be in all other proporcions contryved and fashioned like
vnto the Stadge of the saide Plaie howse called the Globe; With convenient windowes
and lightes glazed to the saide Tyreinge howse; And the saide fframe, Stadge and Stearecases to be covered with Tyle, and to haue a sufficient gutter of lead to carrie & convey
the water frome the coveringe of the saide Stadge to fall backwardes; And also all the

saide fframe and the Staircases thereof to be sufficyently enclosed withoute with lathe,
lyme & haire, and the gentlemens roomes and Twoe pennie roomes to be seeled with
lathe, lyme & haire, and all the fflowers of the saide Galleries, Stories and Stadge to be
bourded with good & sufficyent newe deale bourdes of the whole thicknes, wheare need
shalbe; And the saide howse and other thinges beforemencioned to be made & doen to
be in all other contrivitions, conveyances, fashions, thinge and thinges effected, finished
and doen according to the manner and fashion of the saide howse called the Globe,
saveinge only that all the princypall and maine postes of the saide fframe and Stadge forwarde shalbe square and wroughte palasterwise, with carved proporcions called Satiers
to be placed & sett on the topp of every of the same postes, and saveinge alsoe that the
said Peeter Streete shall not be chardged with anie manner of pay[ntin]ge in or aboute
the saide fframe howse or Stadge or anie parte thereof, nor rendringe the walls within,

nor seeling anie more or other roomes then the gentlemens roomes, Twoe pennie roomes and Stadge before remembred. Nowe theiruppon the saide Peeter Streete dothe covenant, promise and graunte ffor himself, his executours and administratours, to and with the saide Phillipp Henslowe and Edward Allen and either of them, and thexecutours and administratours of them and either of them, by theis presentes in manner & forme followeinge (that is to saie); That he the saide Peeter Streete, his executours or assignes, shall & will att his or their owne propper costes & chardges well, woorkmanlike & substancyallie make, erect, sett upp and fully finishe in and by all thinges, accordinge to the true meaninge of theis presentes, with good, stronge and substancyall newe tymber and other necessarie stuff, all the saide fframe and other woorkes whatsoever in and vppon the saide plott or parcell of grounde (beinge not by anie aucthoretie restrayned, and haveinge ingres, egres & regres to doe the same) before the ffyue & twentith daie of Julie next commeinge after the date hereof; And shall alsoe at his or theire like costes and chardges provide and finde all manner of woorkmen, tymber, joystes, rafters, boordes, dores, boltes, hinges, brick, tyle, lathe, lyme, haire, sande, nailes, lade, iron, glasse, woorkmanshipp and other thinges whatsoever, which shalbe needefull, convenyent & necessarie for the saide fframe & woorkes & euerie parte thereof; And shall alsoe make all the saide fframe in every poynte for Scantlinges lardger and bigger in assize then the Scantlinges of the timber of the saide newe erected howse called the Globe; And alsoe that he the saide Peeter Streete shall furthwith, aswell by himself as by suche other and soemanie woorkmen as shalbe convenient & necessarie, enter into and vppon the saide buildinges and woorkes, and shall in reasonable manner proceede therein withoute anie wilfull detraccion vntill the same shalbe fully effected and finished. In consideracion of all which buildinges and of all stuff & woorkemanshipp thereto belonginge, the saide Phillipp Henslowe & Edward Allen and either of them, ffor themselues, theire, and either of theire executours & administratours, doe joynctlie & seuerallie covenante & graunte to & with the saide Peeter Streete, his executours & administratours by theis presentes, that they the saide Phillipp Henslowe & Edward Allen or one of them, or the executours administratours or assignes of them or one of them, shall & will well & truelie paie or cawse to be paide vnto the saide Peeter Streete, his executours or assignes, att the place aforesaid appoynted for the erectinge of the saide fframe, the full somme of Fower hundred & Fortie Poundes of lawfull money of Englande in manner & forme followeinge (that is to saie), att suche tyme and when as the Tymberwoork of the saide fframe shalbe rayzed & sett upp by the saide Peeter Streete his executours or assignes, or within seaven daies then next followeinge, Twoe hundred & Twentie poundes, and att suche time and when as the saide fframe & woorkes shalbe fullie effected & ffynished as is aforesaide, or within seaven daies then next followeinge, thother Twoe hundred and Twentie poundes, withoute fraude or coven. Prouided allwaies, and it is agreed betwene the saide parties, that whatsoever somme or sommes of money the saide Phillipp Henslowe & Edward Allen or either of them, or thexecutours or assignes of them or either of them, shall lend or deliver vnto the saide Peter Streete his executours or assignes, or anie other by his appoyntemente or consent, ffor or concerninge the saide woorkes or anie parte thereof or anie stuff thereto belonginge, before the razeinge & settinge upp of the saide fframe, shalbe reputed, accepted, taken & accoumpted in parte of the firste paymente aforesaid of the saide some of Fower hundred & Fortie poundes, and all suche somme & sommes of money, as they or anie of them shall as aforesaid lend or deliver betwene the razeinge of the saide fframe & finishinge thereof and of all the rest of the saide woorkes, shalbe reputed, accepted, taken & accoumpted in parte of the laste pamente aforesaid of the same somme of Fower hundred & Fortie poundes, anie thinge abouesaid to the contrary notwithstandinge. In witnes whereof the parties abouesaid to theis presente Indentures Interchaungeably haue sett theire handes and seales. Yeoven the daie and yeare ffirste abouewritten.

P S

Sealed and deliuered by the saide Peter Streete in the presence of me William Harris Pub[lic] Scr[ivener] And me Frauncis Smyth appr[entice] to the said Scr[ivener]

[Endorsed:] Peater Streat ffor The Building of the Fortune.

APPENDIX G

THE CONTRACT FOR BUILDING
THE HOPE THEATRE, 1613

(From the text given by Dr. W. W. Greg in *Henslowe Papers*)

Articles, Covenauntes, grauntes, and agreementes, Concluded and agreed vppon this Nyne and Twenteithe daie of Auguste, Anno Domini 1613, Betwene Phillipe Henslowe of the parishe of St Saviour in Sowthworke within the countye of Surrey, Esquire, and Jacobe Maide of the parishe of St Olaves in Sowthworke aforesaide, waterman, of thone partie, And Gilbert Katherens of the saide parishe of St Saviour in Sowthworke, Carpenter, on thother partie, As followeth, That is to saie—

Inprimis the saide Gilbert Katherens for him, his executours, administratours, and assignes, dothe convenaunt, promise, and graunt to and with the saide Phillipe Henslowe and Jacobe Maide and either of them, thexecutors, administratours, & assigns of them and either of them, by theise presentes in manner and forme following: That he the saied Gilbert Katherens, his executours, administratours, or assignes shall and will, at his or theire owne proper costes and charges, vppon or before the last daie of November next ensuinge the daie of the date of theise presentes above written, not onlie take downe or pull downe all that same place or house wherin Beares and Bulls haue been heretofore vsuallie bayted, and also one other house or staple wherin Bulls and horsses did vsuallie stande, sett, lyinge, and beinge vppon or neere the Banksyde in the saide parishe of St Saviour in Sowthworke, comonlie called or knowne by the name of the Beare garden, but shall also at his or theire owne proper costes and charges vppon or before the saide laste daie of November newly erect, builde, and sett vpp one other same place or Plaiehouse fitt & convenient in all thinges, bothe for players to playe in, and for the game of Beares and Bulls to be bayted in the same, and also a fitt and convenient Tyre house and a stage to be carryed or taken awaie, and to stande vppon tressells good, substanciall, and sufficient for the carryinge and bearinge of suche a stage; And shall new builde, erect, and sett vp againe the saide plaie house or game place neere or vppon the saide place, where the saide game place did heretofore stande; And to builde the same of suche large compasse, fforme, widenes, and height as the Plaie house called the Swan in the libertie of Parris garden in the saide parishe of St Saviour now is; And shall also builde two stearecasses without and adioyninge to the saide Playe house in suche convenient places, as shalbe moste fitt and convenient for the same to stande vppon, and of such largnes and height as the stearecasses of the saide playehouse called the Swan nowe are or bee; And shall also builde the Heavens all over the saide stage, to be borne or carryed without any postes or supporters to be fixed or sett vppon the saide stage, and all gutters of leade needfull for the carryage of all suche raine water as shall fall vppon the same; And shall also make two Boxes in the lowermost storie fitt and decent for gentlemen to sitt in; And shall make the particions betwne the Rommes as they are at the saide Plaie house called the Swan; And to make turned cullumes vppon and over the stage; And shall make the principalls and fore fronte of the saide Plaie house of good and sufficient oken tymber, and no furr tymber to be putt or vsed in the lower most, or midell stories, except the vpright postes on the backparte of the saide stories (all the byndinge joystes to be of oken tymber); The inner principall postes of the first storie to be twelve footes in height and tenn ynches square, the inner principall postes in the midell storie to be eight ynches square, the inner most postes in the vpper storie to be seaven ynches square; The prick postes in the first storie to be eight ynches square, in the seconde storie seaven ynches square, and in the vpper most storie six ynches square; Also the brest sommers in the lower moste storie to be nyne ynches depe, and seaven ynches in thicknes, and in the midell storie to be eight ynches depe and six ynches in thicknes; The byndinge jostes of the firste storie to be nyne and eight ynches in depthe and thicknes, and in the midell storie to be viij and vij ynches in depthe and thicknes. Item to make a good, sure, and sufficient foundacion of brickes for the saide Play house or game place, and to make it xiij^{teene} ynches at the leaste above the grounde. Item to new builde, erect, and sett vpp the saide Bull house and stable with good and sufficient scantlinge tymber, plankes, and bordes, and particions of that largnes and fittnes as shalbe sufficient to kepe and holde six bulls and three horsses or geldinges, with rackes and mangers to the same, and also a lofte or storie over the saide house as nowe it is. And shall also at his & theire owne proper costes and charges new tyle with Englishe tyles all the vpper rooffe of the saide Plaie house, game place, and Bull house or stable, and shall fynde and paie for at his like proper costes and charges for all the lyme, heare, sande, brickes, tyles, lathes, nayles, workemanshipe and all other thinges needfull and necessarie for the full finishinge of the saide Plaie house, Bull house, and stable; And the saide Plaiehouse or game place to be made in althinges and in suche forme and fashion, as the saide plaie house called the Swan (the scantling of the tymbers, tyles, and foundacion as ys aforesaide without fraude or coven). And the saide Phillipe Henslow and Jacobe Maide and either of them for them, thexecutors, administratours, and assignes of them and either of them, doe covenant and graunt to and with the saide Gilbert Katherens, his executours, administratours, and assignes in manner and forme followinge (That is to saie) That he the saide Gilbert or his assignes shall or maie haue, and take to his or theire vse and behoofe, not onlie all the tymber, benches, seates, slates, tyles, brickes, and all other thinges belonginge to the saide Game place & Bull house or stable, and also all suche olde tymber whiche the saide Phillipe Henslow hathe latelie bought, beinge of an old house in Thames street, London, whereof moste parte is now lyinge in the yarde or backsyde of the saide Bearegarden; And also to satisfie and paie vnto the saide Gilbert Katherens, his executors, administratours, or assignes for the doinge and finishinges of the workes and buildinges aforesaid the somme of Three Hundered and three score poundes of good and lawffull monie of England, in manner and forme followinge (That is to saie) In hande at thensealinge and deliuery hereof, Three score pounds which the saide Gilbert acknowlegeth him selfe by theise presentes to haue receaued; And more over to paie every weeke weeklie, duringe the firste six weekes, vnto the saide Gilbert or his assignes, when he shall sett workemen to worke vppon or about the buildinge of the premisses the somme of Tenne poundes of lawffull monie of Englande to paie them there wages (yf theire wages dothe amount vnto somuche monie); And when the saide plaie house, Bull house, and stable are reared, then to make vpp the saide wages one hundered poundes of lawffull monie of England, and to be paide to the saide Gilbert or his assignes; And when the saide Plaie house, Bull house, and stable are Reared, tyled, walled, then to paie vnto the saide Gilbert Katherens or his assignes one other hundred poundes of lawffull monie of England; And when the saide Plaie house, Bull house, and stable are fullie finished, builded, and done in manner and forme aforesaide, then to paie vnto the saide Gilbert Katherens or his assignes one other hundred Poundes of lawffull monie of England in full satisfacion and payment of the saide somme of CClx^{ll}. And to all and singuler the covenantes, grauntes, articles, and agreementes above in theise presentes contayned, whiche on the parte and behalfe of the saide Gilbert Katherens, his executours, administratours, or assignes are ought to be observed, performed, fulfilled, and done, the saide Gilbert Katherens byndeth himselfe, his executours, administratours, and assignes vnto the saide Phillipe Henslowe and Jacob Maide and to either of them, thexecutours, administratours, and assignes of them or either of them, by theise presentes. In witnes whereof the saide Gilbert Katherens hath herevnto sett his hande and seale, the daie and yere firste above written

The mark G K of Gilbert Katherens

Sealed and Deliuered in the presence of

witnes Moyses Bowler

Edwarde Griffin

Index

THIS BOOK IS SET IN MONOTYPE BEMBO
AND PRINTED IN GREAT BRITAIN BY
RICHARD CLAY AND COMPANY LIMITED
BUNGAY SUFFOLK